"I Have A Dress For You," He Declared.

"I'd prefer to wear my own clothes," she told him.

"And I'd prefer you to wear the dress I selected."

"I think we're at a stalemate," she said.

"No, we're not."

"We're not?" she asked. She shook her head. "I know you think you're going to get your way, but—"

"I don't think it, Bella. I *know* it. Because as my mistress, you'll put my preferences first."

Dear Reader,

I'm a native Floridian born in South Florida. During the turbulent early 70s, my family left Miami and moved farther north, first to Fort Pierce and then eventually to Lake Alfred. But my maternal grandparents moved only as far as Okeechobee and settled there.

As a young girl I would visit them. My grandmother would always plan a special shopping day for my mom, my sisters and me. A day that involved driving to West Palm Beach and Palm Beach and shopping at the luxury stores.

When I sat down to write this book, I was missing Florida as I always do! And I started to think about locations. Visiting the ritzy Palm Beach area was always fun for me, because my grandmother would buy us something and we'd have adventures. Then I thought about what it would be like to live there and *not* have money.

Or…to have money and lose it all. And then Bella was born in my imagination. I knew immediately that her hero had to be someone who was a part of the world that she no longer belonged to. I knew that he had to be someone who had something she wanted—besides his hunky physique. And I knew that there would be some scandal from her past to overcome. I hope you enjoy the luxury and drama of *Six-Month Mistress!*

Please stop by my Web site at www.katherinegarbera.com for a behind-the-scenes look into *Six-Month Mistress*.

Happy reading!

Katherine

KATHERINE GARBERA

SIX-MONTH MISTRESS

Published by Silhouette Books
America's Publisher of Contemporary Romance

SILHOUETTE BOOKS

ISBN-13: 978-0-373-76802-8
ISBN-10:   0-373-76802-8

SIX-MONTH MISTRESS

Copyright © 2007 by Katherine Garbera

All rights reserved. Except for use in any review, the reproduction
or utilization of this work in whole or in part in any form by any
electronic, mechanical or other means, now known or hereafter
invented, including xerography, photocopying and recording, or in
any information storage or retrieval system, is forbidden without
the written permission of the editorial office, Silhouette Books,
233 Broadway, New York, NY 10279 U.S.A.

This is a work of fiction. Names, characters, places and incidents are
either the product of the author's imagination or are used fictitiously, and
any resemblance to actual persons, living or dead, business establishments,
events or locales is entirely coincidental.

This edition published by arrangement with Harlequin Books S.A.

® and TM are trademarks of Harlequin Books S.A., used under license.
Trademarks indicated with ® are registered in the United States Patent
and Trademark Office, the Canadian Trade Marks Office and in other
countries.

Visit Silhouette Books at www.eHarlequin.com

Printed in U.S.A.

Recent Books by Katherine Garbera

Silhouette Desire

*In Bed with Beauty #1535
*Cinderella's Christmas Affair #1546
*Let It Ride #1558
Sin City Wedding #1567
*Mistress Minded #1587
*Rock Me All Night #1672
†His Wedding-Night Wager #1708
†Her High-Stakes Affair #1714
†Their Million-Dollar Night #1720
The Once-A-Mistress Wife #1749
**Make-Believe Mistress #1798
**Six-Month Mistress #1802

Silhouette Bombshell

Exposed #10
Night Life #23
The Amazon Strain #43
Exclusive #94

*King of Hearts
†What Happens in Vegas…
**The Mistresses

KATHERINE GARBERA

is a strong believer in happily ever after. She found her own after meeting her Prince Charming in Fantasyland at Walt Disney World. She's written more than thirty books and has been nominated for a *Romantic Times BOOKreviews* career achievement award in Series Fantasy and Series Adventure respectively. Katherine recently moved to the Dallas area where she lives with her husband and their two children. Visit Katherine on the Web at www.katherinegarbera.com.

This book is dedicated to my sisters...
Donna and Linda sisters by birth. Nancy, Mary Louise,
Eve and Beverly sisters by chance.

One

"Jeremy Harper is here to see you."

"Send him in," Isabella McNamara said, even though he wasn't on her calendar. She hung up the phone and settled back in her leather executive chair, blowing out a long breath. This was just another meeting. She faced heads of Fortune 500 companies all the time—facing Jeremy would be no different.

Yeah, right.

She wiped her sweaty palms on the fabric of her silk skirt and immediately regretted it. She wanted to look her best, to pull off some of Angelina Jolie's charm and confidence. Taking a deep breath, she repeated a few words in her head—calm, cool, clever.

Everything was always different with Jeremy. She'd seen him exactly twelve times in the last three years. And each of those meetings had left her shaken, hungry and wanting more of the man. Of course, since she'd pretty much signed away her body to him, every time they'd met all she could think about was what it would be like to feel his naked skin rubbing against hers.

Oh, God, he'd turned her into a sex fiend. She knew that being a man's mistress wasn't about sex; it was about money. But Bella had never been able to think of anything to do with Jeremy as only business.

She didn't have to guess why he was here. Three short years ago, she'd made a deal with Jeremy and now it was time to pay up. She didn't kid herself that he was here for any reason other than to collect on that debt.

The door to her office opened and she stood to greet him. He wore a Dolce & Gabbana suit with the same ease that teenagers wore jeans and T-shirts. He sauntered into the room as if he owned it.

She caught her breath, wishing for a minute she didn't find him so attractive. But she always had. And that was probably why she was in the position she was: Owing this man a debt she had no idea if she would survive paying.

The door closed firmly behind him, but she

barely noticed. Instead she tried to ignore the spicy scent of his aftershave and the way his bluer-than-blue eyes watched her.

He was her devil. The man she'd sold her soul to—and he was here to collect. She twisted her fingers together, trying desperately to believe that she wasn't scared of a six-foot-two man. But she was.

"Hello, Bella."

His voice was deep and low-pitched. She'd spoken to him on the phone countless times, yet his voice always sent little shivers of awareness pulsing through her veins.

"Jeremy," she said, then remembered a very important lesson that her mother had taught her. *Never let them see you sweat.* Of course, her mom had been referring to the Palm Beach jet set they'd once been a part of, but Bella figured the same rule applied to sexy billionaires. "Please have a seat."

He moved farther into the room, seating himself in one of her guest chairs. She sank down into her leather chair, opening her center desk drawer and touching the jewel-encrusted Montblanc fountain pen that had once been her mother's and was now Bella's lucky charm. She rubbed her fingers over it before taking it out of the drawer and placing it on the desk.

"What can I do for you?" she asked carefully. He might be here for another reason. Maybe he wanted her to cater an event for his company or his family's annual Fourth of July bash.

"I think you know."

She sighed. Not an event after all. "Time's up."

He laughed, a rich sound that filled the room, and for a moment she forgot to be afraid. Forgot that he held all the cards in this situation by her own design.

"I was hoping time would have helped alleviate your fears."

"I'm not afraid of you," she said, very aware that her words were a lie.

She didn't care if Jeremy knew it, either. She'd spent most of her life dealing with people she was afraid of, ever since her father had died when she was fourteen and they'd gotten the news that his entire fortune was gone. She'd learned to deal with the fear of being mocked by the same people she'd once called friends.

She'd faced fear again when her mother died four years later and the sole responsibility for raising her fourteen-year-old brother, Dare, had fallen to her. She'd known real fear—survival fear—and she'd never once admitted to it out loud.

Jeremy arched one eyebrow at her—an arrogant gesture that fit him to a tee.

She forced a smile. "Dare is still in college."

"He's graduating at the end of summer. And he has a job lined up with Fidelity starting in the fall."

"How do you know that?" she asked. Dare had only just called this afternoon with the job news. She'd known then that she needed to call Jeremy.

To let him know that she was now ready to fulfill her part of the bargain.

"I told you I'd make sure your brother's future was taken care of."

"I thought you meant the scholarship." But she'd suspected he'd done more. Dare had mentioned a few times that Jeremy had visited him at school.

He shook his head. "I'm not here to discuss your brother."

No, of course he wasn't. He was here to discuss her and the contract she'd signed three years ago. A contract in which she'd agreed to be his mistress for six months in return for the help he'd given both her and her brother.

"So, it starts tonight?" she asked at last. For three years he'd been waiting for her to be free of her obligation to her brother. For three years she'd seen him every three months to affirm that the deal was still on. For three years she'd dreamed of his passionate embraces…and the hope that, once they started their affair, she'd be able to convince him that she was meant to be more than his mistress. Because she wanted to be Jeremy's wife.

"I believe you're free," he said.

She was available tonight. The new manager she'd hired had proven himself capable of handling all the events, so she was taking a rare night off. How did he know? "Did Dare tell you?"

"He didn't have to. I asked your assistant."

"You're a very thorough man." She was going to have a talk with Shelley about giving out personal information. Her hands were shaking and she clenched them together so he wouldn't notice. He was just a man. But for some reason he'd always been more to her.

"When I see something I want…" he said.

"And you want me?"

"After the kisses we've shared, I know you don't doubt that."

She didn't. But by the same token, she'd always sort of wished she'd just imagined the intensity in Jeremy's eyes when he looked at her.

She had no real idea how to respond to that. "Um…I…"

He stood up and walked around her desk to stand next to her chair. She tipped her head back to look up at him. "Changed your mind?"

She couldn't read the emotion in his eyes—there wasn't any. For all the reaction she saw, he might not care either way. And that was why she was afraid. She'd been desperate when she'd agreed to the contract, wanting to stop feeling so alone in the world. People she knew left but, if she had the chance, she knew she could convince Jeremy to stay.

Jeremy had gone beyond what he'd said he would do, introducing her to business partners of his and recommending her party-planning services before she had any real references. He'd helped tremendously to get her business off the ground, and to ensure its success.

And she wanted him, she did. She was just afraid that the secret crush she'd always had on him would make it too easy for her to believe there was something more between them than a contract.

She was attracted to Jeremy. She'd been in lust with him since she'd first met him when she was sixteen. She'd been working at the Palm Beach Yacht Club as a waitress and he'd been dining with a bunch of his college friends. He'd been tan and fit and incredibly handsome. And polite—the nicest to her by far.

When he'd finally approached her a few years later, she'd been thrilled at first. Until she realized that what he was offering was a business arrangement. An arrangement that she'd never regretted not turning down.

"I haven't changed my mind. I gave you my word." She didn't feel guilty about the contract she'd signed. A lot of women married for money and then divorced and married again. In essence she was doing the same thing.

"And your word is your bond?"

"It has to be. I didn't have anything else when you made your offer." She didn't like to remember those days, the despair and the sense of failure that she'd been mired in.

"You had your pride," he said softly, running one finger down the side of her face. He cupped her jaw in his hand and she held her breath.

His gaze fell to her mouth and stayed there. She licked her dry lips and his gaze narrowed. Silly as it sounded, she could feel his eyes on her lips.

"I still do."

"Good."

She leaned away from him. "It would make me feel more comfortable if everything you said didn't sound so arrogant."

"I can't help that."

"You can, you just choose not to."

"I've had thirty-four years to get this way."

"And no one has ever complained?"

"Not to my face."

"I don't think I'm going to be able to keep my comments to myself."

"I wouldn't want you to. I'm not asking you to pretend to be someone you aren't."

But he was. The woman she was today was different from the one she'd been three years ago. And at twenty-six she wasn't sure she could pretend they were dating when she knew the truth. That she was his mistress. That the relationship was stamped with an expiration date. And that he was planning to walk away from her without looking back or leaving any of his emotions behind.

* * *

Jeremy stared down into Bella's big brown eyes and felt like he'd taken a punch to the gut. He'd waited lifetimes for this night. True, he knew it had been only three years, but they seemed long—too long. His skin felt too tight and if she didn't lose the nervous look, he wasn't sure what he was going to do.

She was his. For the last three years that knowledge had been in the back of his mind. His life had gone the same as always. But in the back of his mind he knew that Bella McNamara belonged to him. Finally he could claim her.

He had a contract with her signature on it. A legal document that proclaimed she'd be his mistress for six months. But even he wasn't that big of a bastard—he wouldn't force Bella into his arms and his bed if she didn't want to be there.

Still, he'd have absolutely no qualms about seducing her into his bed. About using the passion that had always been between them to gain her acceptance and get her where he wanted her.

"Um…how is this going to work? Will we go to your place right now?" she asked. A strand of her hair had escaped the clip at the back and curled against her cheek. She tucked it behind her ear absently.

She bit her lower lip. Her mouth was full and enticing. It was the second thing he'd noticed about her. He had tasted her lips before, when he'd held her in his arms. But the way he felt about her was…hell, he couldn't define what he felt for her. He wanted to groan out loud.

"No, not now. We're attending the Tristan-Andrew Cancer Institute charity benefit tonight. Our arrangement will stay private. In public, it will seem like we're dating."

"Thank you," she said.

"For?"

"For keeping our arrangement private. I don't really want the world to know," she said, her words breathy. A soft little confession.

Jeremy didn't pretend he understood women but he did know that socially a girlfriend and a mistress weren't in the same league. He'd seen that firsthand with his own father's women. Bella had enough marks against her socially. But this was the only arrangement she would accept from him. And mistresses he understood.

He'd hoped for a different sort of evening—an intimate dinner for two on his yacht, followed by dancing under the stars. But at least at the charity benefit there would be music and he could hold her in his arms.

The last three years had been the longest of his life. He hadn't been celibate, but every woman he'd slept with had become Bella in his head. He wanted *her*. When he woke in the morning he imagined her soft brown eyes opening to meet his. She'd become an obsession—and a successful businessman couldn't afford to be obsessed with anything other than business.

She licked her lips again and his body clenched. He wanted to know the taste of her mouth. It had been too long since he'd last kissed her. This time he did groan out loud.

"What?"

He shrugged. The safe bet would be to play it off as not wanting to go to the charity event. He liked social events, normally. Tonight he was being generous in letting her have this time to adjust to being in a relationship with him.

The event had been organized by his mother. His family was a major benefactor to the local cancer institute. They were hosting the charity fashion event this evening at Neiman Marcus. His mother had called to remind him that plenty of single ladies would be in attendance, all of them suitable to become Mrs. Jeremy Harper III.

Which made this the perfect night to be seen with Bella.

He rubbed the back of his neck to keep from reaching out and capturing that strand of hair that was once again curled against her cheek. "Are you familiar with the event?"

"We lost the bid to cater it." She said it almost absently. She straightened some papers on her desk and only then did he notice the fine trembling of her hand.

"Forget about your business for one night," he said, trying to process her reaction. His own hands shook at the thought of being alone with her. The feelings she evoked in him were that intense.

"I don't think that's a good idea."

"Why not?" he asked.

"Business is all we have between us," she said, staring up at him. He knew he was missing something in the words and her expression, but he couldn't figure out what it was. If it *was* just business between them, then he couldn't have her. He never wanted to be more involved than his partner in an intimate relationship.

"Our business is very personal," he said at last, capturing that curl and wrapping it around his finger. It was what he wanted to do with her. Wrap himself in her curvy body and silky limbs.

"Yes, it is. And, oh God, I'm not sure—"

He covered her mouth with his fingers. Her lips were plump and moist from her breath. "You can change your mind."

She shook her head. "I don't want to."

He smiled then, hoping his relief didn't show. It was unnerving to be so attracted to a woman. He'd jumped through hoops for Bella that he wouldn't have for any other woman. After all, he'd waited three years for her.

"Then let's go to the party and see where the night leads."

"What about the contract?" she asked, clearly still uneasy with him.

He struggled for a way to put her at ease. He knew he could be charming, but with Bella he wasn't his usual self. From the moment he'd suggested that she become his mistress, he'd been out of control.

At the time she'd seemed so young—only twenty-three—and so fragile.

"We can discuss it over dinner after the party," he said. He wasn't ready to let her out of the contract. He knew a better man would have torn the document up a long time ago, but frankly it was the only leverage he had with Bella. Leverage he didn't want to let go of.

"Okay. I can have my secretary make us a reservation," she said, trying to take control of the situation.

He held back a smile. He admired her bid for power but there was no way he was letting her take charge. "I'll take care of that. Just get your purse or briefcase and we can leave."

"Leave?" she asked. Her face flushed and she looked like she wanted to tell him off. Finally he felt like they were getting somewhere. He saw the real Bella in that instant. The woman he'd first been attracted to. The woman of passion and pride and determination. Not someone who was biddable and afraid of him, something he didn't want.

"Yes. My driver is waiting out front."

She smiled sweetly at him. "Thanks for the offer of a ride, but I have to go home and get changed."

"I have a dress for you."

"That's nice, but I'd prefer to wear my own clothes."

"And I'd prefer you to wear the dress I selected."

"I think we're at a stalemate."

"No, we're not."

"We're not?"

"No."

She shook her head. "I know you think you're going to get your way, but—"

"I don't think it, Bella, I know it."

"Why?"

"Because as my mistress you'll put my preferences first."

Two

Bella laced her fingers together under the desk to keep from doing something she was sure she'd regret. She wished she had a mentor when it came to filling the role of a mistress, but she didn't. She sensed it would be easier to just let her pride go. *Once you agree to be a man's mistress, your pride means nothing.*

If only. Suddenly it wasn't the sex that concerned her, but the attitude that she'd have to pretend to have. She tried to smile, but couldn't force herself. If only she owed him money, then she could go to the bank and take out a loan, but he'd given her a lot more than money. He'd given her contacts, business advice and provided a male role model for Dare. Those were things that couldn't be paid back in dollars.

"This isn't going to work. I'm sorry that I didn't realize it before, but I'm not the kind of woman who can—"

He put his fingers over her lips again. Her tongue brushed his skin for a second before she closed her mouth, staring up at him.

She felt her resolve melting and it had absolutely nothing to do with not wanting to be in breach of the contract she'd signed. It had to do with his eyes.

His touch was featherlight and almost tentative. Like he wasn't sure he had the right to touch her, but couldn't help himself. That reassured her. No matter what he'd said before, there was more to this than a contract.

He must know he was pushing her. Did he want her to renege? Had that been his plan all along? She wanted to take his arrogance down a peg or two.

She had no idea how to handle herself with him. He had something she wanted. Something he *knew* she wanted. That elusive stamp of approval from the crowd that had tossed her out without a backward glance—and the only sure way to get that back was to marry into the crowd. And she was willing to do anything to make that happen.

If she had to swallow her pride and her temper, then she would. Being a mistress should be easy enough. She had to do nothing but live for pleasure and smile at her man. Make him feel like he was the sexiest, smartest, wealthiest man in the room.

God, she didn't think she could do it. Even for the chance to walk into a room with him, that most elusive of men, the ultimate bachelor. A man whom every single woman in that elite social jet set wanted to claim. And she thought—no, knew—she could win him over for a lifetime.

It was small and petty, but that thought made her tip her head to the side and smile up at him. "Of course, I'll wear the dress you selected."

"Let's go then."

"I'll need a few minutes to get ready. I'll meet you in the waiting room."

He nodded and walked out of the room. She collapsed into her chair as soon as he was gone.

There was a brief knock on the door and then it opened again.

"Bella?"

"Yes, Shelley?"

"He asked me to give you this."

Shelley handed her a small, gold-foil-wrapped box. "I had no idea the two of you were dating."

And so it starts. "We've known each other for years."

"I know that. Are you going to open it?"

She didn't want to know what was inside. A gift for a mistress might be different than a gift for a girlfriend. She thought maybe she should open it by herself, but Shelley didn't look like she was leaving. Her assistant was also the closest thing that Bella had to a friend.

"Yes, I'll open it."

She didn't let herself dwell on the fact that it had been almost ten years since she'd received a wrapped present. Dare gave her gifts, but generally left them in the bag from the store they'd come from. She slipped the ribbon off the box and set it aside.

"Oh, man, I can't wait to see what it is. How can you go so slowly?"

"I don't get that many gifts."

"Me neither. Not like this. Not from men."

Bella slipped her fingernail under the seam in the paper and ripped it away. The box was long and narrow, and when the paper fell away she saw it was that distinctive Tiffany blue. *Jewelry*. He'd gotten her jewelry.

Shelley perched her hip on the desk and leaned forward as Bella lifted the lid. It was a platinum, diamond-encrusted choker.

Shelley gasped a little and reached out to touch it. "It's gorgeous."

"Yes, it is," Bella said. She realized that he'd done her a favor, insisting she wear a dress he'd purchased. She would have worn one of her mother's old haute couture dresses and costume jewelry and all the time she'd have felt like a fraud.

Did he realize that? Or had buying her a dress and, she assumed, a wardrobe simply been part of preparing her to be his?

She closed the jewelry box and slipped it into her leather Coach bag. She'd skimped and saved until she could afford the large, classy bag that she wanted and needed for work.

Her stomach was still a knot of nerves, but she refused to think about it. Instead she fell back on her business. "Remind Randall to call me when the event tonight is over. I want to know how it went."

"Are you sure about that?"

"Of course I'm sure."

"If I was going out with someone like Jeremy Harper I wouldn't want my phone ringing."

"Shelley…"

"None of my business, I know. Have fun tonight, boss lady."

Bella knew she'd have a lot of things tonight and wasn't sure fun was one of them. But she was excited and nervous and a million other things that she'd never expected. It wasn't just Jeremy. It was her return to Palm Beach society and the ten long years it had taken to get there.

Jeremy escaped from his partner's spouse, who desperately wanted to find him a wife. Despite the fact that he'd arrived tonight with Bella on his arm, Lucinda wasn't deterred. She had a friend she wanted him hooked up with and nothing would stop her.

Ever since Daniel and Lucinda had married, Lucinda Cannon-Posner had been trying to pair him up with her oh-so-proper society friends. The moment Bella had stepped away to powder her nose, Lucinda and her friend Marianne had pounced.

Jeremy eased deeper into the shadows, waiting for Bella to reappear. He was surprised by how much he was enjoying the evening. Normally these events were a total bore. But tonight, with Bella at his side, he'd been enjoying himself—until Lucinda and her friend had made their move.

"Hiding from Marianne?"

Jeremy glanced over at Kell Ottenberg. He and his cousin had been best friends forever. Their mothers were sisters and the two men had been raised together. Kell handed him a martini glass.

"Waiting for Bella."

"Ah, the mystery lady. Rumor has it she's been hired for the evening."

Jeremy knew Kell was trying to get a rise out of him. The fact that he'd hit so close to the mark was something Jeremy chose to ignore. "You're the one who has to pay for companionship."

"I don't have to pay, but it does make life easier. None of those messy entanglements that come from getting involved."

Jeremy shrugged. Kell had a bad attitude toward

women and it was understandable. He'd been raked over the coals by a first-class, gold-plated bitch.

"So who is she?"

"Isabella McNamara," Jeremy said. Kell leaned back against the wall. The fashion show was going on next door and this room was relatively quiet.

"Where did you find her?" Kell asked.

"Hiding." She'd been living in a small duplex in Fort Pierce. Not that many miles from Palm Beach, but a world away.

"Ah, so that's what you two have in common."

Jeremy punched Kell on the arm. "I'm not hiding, I'm waiting."

Kell glanced around the area. "In the corner?"

Jeremy shrugged.

"Why don't you tell Daniel to have a talk with Lucinda?"

"I have. He doesn't want to upset her."

"After seven years of marriage he shouldn't be so concerned about that."

Jeremy knew from observing Daniel with his wife that he loved Lucinda and he'd do anything to keep her happy. Frankly, Jeremy didn't understand Daniel and Lucinda's relationship. His own parents had been happiest apart. His father had always kept a mistress on the side and everyone had seemed pleased with that arrangement.

"She is beautiful," Kell said.

"Marianne? I'll tell Lucinda you think so."

"No, thanks. I meant your lady," Kell said, gesturing to Bella, who was walking slowly toward them. She glanced up, caught him watching her and smiled.

"Later."

"Later? Don't I get to meet her?"

"I'm taking her to the dance floor. I think three would be a crowd."

"I'll just cut in."

Jeremy glanced at his friend. "Why?"

"I want to meet her."

He knew from Kell's tone that he wanted to question her. "She's not like—"

"I'm sure she's not. I'll be good, I promise."

"Somehow I doubt that," Jeremy said under his breath.

He went to meet her, aware that Kell was only a few steps behind him. Jeremy cupped his hand under her elbow and drew her away from the fashion show into a third room where the DJ and dance floor were set up, ready for the party to spill over once the fashion show ended.

"I'm sorry if I kept you waiting," she said.

"No problem." He heard Kell chuckle behind him and suspected it was because he sounded like an idiot. What the hell was it about this woman that made his brain short circuit?

He'd dated beautiful women before, so it wasn't that. There was something else about her. The dress he'd selected was perfect for her. It was a summer cocktail dress with a slim-fitting skirt and a scoop neck.

"Hello, Isabella," Kell said, reaching past him and offering her his hand. "I'm Kell."

She took his hand. Kell lifted it to his lips, kissing the back of it and smirking at Jeremy while he did so.

Bella smiled at Kell and Jeremy felt his gut tighten. He knew she was his, and she knew it, too. But he still felt a twinge of jealousy.

"Let's dance," Jeremy said, drawing her away from Kell and tucking her up against his side.

Kell's laughter followed them as they walked away. Jeremy ignored it. He wanted to believe his reaction had absolutely nothing to do with jealousy. She was his mistress for six months, nothing more. He told himself that he only wanted to keep Bella from being hurt by Kell, who could be charming but would never be sincere.

"What was that about?" she asked, a different note in her voice. He glanced down at her and saw the smile lingering at her mouth. She was still nervous, but the exchange with Kell had relaxed her. She was teasing him.

"Kell's a goofball. Don't pay any attention to him," he said.

"You have a friend who's a goofball?"

"Unfortunately, I'm related to him."

"How?"

"Cousins. Our moms are sisters."

"Ah, so the crazy gene…"

He pulled her into his arms as the DJ played a slow song. "Skipped my branch of the family."

"Whatever you say."

He didn't say anything else, just pulled her closer in his arms. She relaxed against him, following his lead. They fit together perfectly.

He kept stroking his hand down her back, completely obliterating her thought process. She liked the strength in his arms. The way they felt wrapped around her.

For a minute Bella bought into the illusion of security that his arms offered. She closed her eyes and let the spicy scent of his aftershave fill each breath she took. The music was slow with a funky beat. With her eyes closed, she could let her worries and fears and the past years drop away.

She could just be Bella and pretend this was her teenage fantasy come to life. She thought she'd known all about Jeremy from her crush those many summers ago, but she was coming to realize there was so much more to the man.

She remembered seeing Kell back then. He and Jeremy were photo negatives of each other, both tall, one blond and outgoing, the other dark and dangerous.

More than once she'd wondered why Jeremy

had made his offer to her. What had he seen in her that had made him offer to help her?

Was it only sex, a desire for her to be his mistress? She looked up and met his gaze. She was surprised that he was watching her. If he was pretending, then he was a better actor than she was. He held her and looked at her like she was his. His for more than six months and because of more than a contract. She knew it was an illusion, but she hoped to make it a reality.

"What?" he asked with a hint of tenderness in his voice.

"Uh…" She couldn't remember what she'd been about to say. She wrapped her arms around his shoulders, let her fingers caress the back of his neck. Held him. This was what she'd dreamed of for the last three years.

Bella realized that giving herself up to Jeremy freed her to just be herself.

He continued to stare down at her, making her wish she could remember what she'd been about to say. She started to worry that something was wrong with the way she looked. She resisted the urge to pat her hair. Oh, man, she hoped she didn't have a bit of spinach in her teeth or something like that. Something that marked her clearly as an outsider. This was the kind of event her mother had missed the most when they'd had to move out of the mansion and into that shabby apartment.

It was odd to Bella that she was actually attending this event and not working it as a caterer—or standing on the sidewalk with her mother, pretending they were window-shopping. A shiver of embarrassment crawled down her spine as she remembered arriving tonight and seeing Lucinda Cannon and friends spot her outside.

"Why me?" she asked, finally remembering what she'd wanted to say.

He brushed his finger down her cheek before he cupped her jaw. His hand enveloped the side of her face, his fingers caressing her neck. His gaze was compelling. She couldn't decipher what she saw in his eyes. He lowered his head until there was barely an inch of space between them.

"You're not like any other woman I know," he said.

That wasn't what she had wanted to hear. She didn't want to be so different that everyone could see it in a glance. She wanted to blend into the moneyed set that she'd partly grown up in. She wanted to forget that she'd ever been cast out and use Jeremy to find her place again. But that wasn't what she was doing tonight.

Instead she was enjoying his arms around her and wishing they were alone. Wishing for a minute that this entire night was real. Wishing he'd asked her because he cared for her, and not because she was going to be his mistress.

This was the very thing that woke her in the middle of the night. How was she going to make Jeremy fall for her? She knew she had to keep him from seeing that she wanted so much more than to be his mistress. Somehow, she had to seduce him into seeing her as more.

"I'm sure of that," she said at last. She *was* different from the other women in the room. She'd had to scrape and struggle to get back to this glitzy world. She doubted even Jeremy understood the toll those years had taken on her.

"I meant it as a compliment," he said, brushing his lips over hers. His lips were full and firm.

All night he'd been touching her. Accustoming her to his touch and taste. The feel of his body brushing against her.

He didn't push his tongue into her mouth, just pressed his lips lightly against hers. Someone cleared his throat, but Jeremy didn't pull away. He lifted his head slowly, caressing her face before he turned to face a man she didn't know.

"I see now why you're avoiding Marianne."

"Who's Marianne?" she asked, trying to calm her racing blood. She didn't like the fact he'd rattled her with that one brief touch of his lips on hers.

Jeremy kept his arm around her waist, but turned them toward the man who'd interrupted them. The music changed again to a more lively number and Jeremy led her off the dance floor.

"One of my wife's friends. I'm Daniel Posner," the man said, following close behind them.

"Isabella McNamara," she said.

"What do you want, Daniel?" Jeremy asked.

"To invite you and your date to join us at our table," he said, gesturing to a round of eight set near the dance floor.

Bella smiled over at the table until she recognized Lucinda Cannon. Her heart started racing and the blood drained from her face. She'd hoped to see Lucinda again, hoped to have the chance to meet her onetime friend as an equal once more. But she wasn't ready yet. It was too soon.

Daniel wrapped his arm around Lucinda as she approached. "This is my wife, Lucinda. Honey, this is Isabella McNamara."

"We know each other," Lucinda said.

Bella could only nod at Lucinda, not sure what to say or how to fill the awkward gap of silence that grew between all four of them.

She pulled away from Jeremy and then realized how cowardly that was. She wasn't at this event as part of the staff. Jeremy glanced down at her. She shook her head, afraid to open her mouth. Afraid she'd blurt out something she didn't want to say.

Jeremy took charge. "We'd love to join you, but we have a dinner reservation and have to leave now. Another time?"

"Certainly. Enjoy your dinner."

The look Lucinda gave Bella before she and Daniel walked away was haughty and telling. And the good feelings Bella had had about being back in this high-society world suddenly dissipated.

Three

No one would ever call him a sensitive man, but even he could tell something was wrong when his date lost all color from her face. While they waited for the valet to bring his convertible Jaguar up, he watched Bella slowly sink deeper and deeper into herself. She wrapped her arms around her waist and kept her eyes down.

The June evening was hot and humid. He pulled Bella to his side and stepped away from the crowd waiting for their cars. She pulled away from him as soon as they were out of the crowd.

"Are you okay?"

"Yes," she said, but he knew she wasn't.

"You're pale as a ghost."

"Can't you just ignore it? I'll be back to normal in a minute."

"No, I can't ignore it. I didn't realize you knew Lucinda."

"Well, I do, and it's been years since I saw her…I thought I'd feel differently."

"How did you feel?"

"What are you, my shrink?"

"I'd like to think I'm your friend." Friend, he thought. Was that really what he wanted?

"I just expected it to be different."

"It?"

His car was brought up, but he signaled the valet that they'd be a minute more. The feeling of protectiveness was disturbing. He wanted to keep her in the safe box labeled *mistress*. He didn't want her upsets to affect him. Yet they did.

"Being back in that room was different," she said, her voice very soft.

He had the feeling she was talking more to herself than to him. For the first time he realized that he wanted more than Bella's body. He wanted her secrets, too.

"Different meaning better?" he asked.

"Not necessarily. I think I may have been feeling a bit vindictive when I imagined it."

He laughed at the way she said that. He already knew she wasn't all sweetness and light. He'd seen her temper and her sheer force of will, both of which she'd used to support herself and her brother.

He cupped her elbow and led her to his car. As he held the door for her and she slid into the seat, the skirt of her dress rose slightly on her thighs. He stared at her leg until she put her hand on the exposed skin and tugged the fabric down.

He closed the door and walked around the car, using the few seconds to regain his control. The entire mistress contract was supposed to enable him to control his feelings around her. Instead he had the feeling that it had backfired on him.

He saw Kell come outside just as he closed the car door. The expression on Kell's face wasn't a good one and he wondered what had happened after they'd left.

He lifted one eyebrow, a silent question to Kell: Should he stay? Kell shook his head and motioned that he'd call later.

Bella fixed her lipstick in the visor mirror and then turned toward him, putting her hand on his thigh.

He glanced at her. It was the first time she'd initiated contact. She scraped her fingernail over the fabric of his pants and he felt that touch echo all the way to his core.

"Thank you," she said.

He had no idea what she was thanking him for, but if she moved her hand a little bit higher she'd see how much he appreciated her touch. He shook his head, trying to clear it.

"For?"

She rubbed his leg one more time and then pulled her hand back. "For pretending you care."

He didn't like the way that sounded.

"I'm not pretending, Bella," he said, capturing her hand and putting it back on his leg. After tonight he hoped she'd have no doubts about how he felt toward her. "I've always cared for you."

She gave him a sideways look and stroked her finger up the inside of his thigh. "Most people don't consider lust caring."

She made him want to laugh at the wry way she said it. It was one of a hundred things about Bella that made him want to be around her. He knew she was scared of any intimacy between them, yet she played that down and treated the attraction with a frankness that was refreshingly honest.

"It's always been more than lust where you're concerned," he said, putting the car in gear and leaving Neiman Marcus behind. And that one crucial point disturbed him more than he thought it would. It was why he'd decided to ask her to be his mistress. His father said that the women who affected a man most deeply were the ones a man had to be careful of.

She said nothing as the miles passed. Then she turned off the radio and reached for his arm.

"Yes?"

"I'm sorry about that. When I'm not sure of myself I can be mean."

"You weren't mean."

"Yes I was. And you were really trying to be nice to me."

"So why did you have a self-confidence attack?"

"Lucinda Cannon," she said, and pulled her hand back to her own side of the car.

Bella knew she was ruining her image, but could only deal with so much at a time. She was losing control of the evening. Losing the perfect bubble that she'd managed to wrap herself in at the charity event.

Pretending she was someone else—a mysterious stranger who belonged—had helped. But one glimpse of Lucinda Cannon had brought her back to herself. Back to the girl who'd been sent home from the exclusive Swedish boarding school for failure to pay her tuition. Back to the girl whose mother had turned to her society friends for help and had volunteered her to clean the homes of people she'd once considered friends.

She could hear Lucinda's pitying words from long ago still echoing in her head. And she knew that this night wasn't about the past. This night was about establishing herself as Jeremy's mistress and securing her future so that she'd never have to endure pitying looks or charity again.

That was one of the reasons she'd signed the mistress contract. She couldn't stand the thought of taking charity from another person. She shook her head to clear it as Jeremy turned off the road and into the parking lot at the public beach.

"What are we doing here?" she asked, trying not to feel relieved that they weren't at a restaurant. She wasn't ready to face anyone, not even strangers. Her reaction to seeing Lucinda had left her raw and exposed and she had no idea how to pull her shell back around her.

Jeremy didn't say a word. He put down the windows and then the top of his car. The moon was only a sliver and stars were visible in the evening sky. It was still light enough to see.

The sound of the rolling waves hitting the shore filled the car as did the warm, ocean-scented breeze. She leaned her head back against the seat and closed her eyes, breathing in nature.

She focused internally as he fiddled with the radio. The mellow sound of the Dave Matthews Band flowed from the speakers. She loved the group and somehow wasn't surprised that Jeremy would know that. He was a thorough man. The kind who noticed details and remembered them.

"I think you need to mellow out," he said, shrugging out of his jacket and tossing it in the backseat. He loosened his tie and unbuttoned the top button of his shirt.

"Mellow out?" she asked. The words were incongruous with Jeremy. He personified hard work and drive. She'd heard his Blackberry beep a couple of times while they'd been driving, and at Neiman Marcus he'd excused himself twice to take calls from his office.

He slanted her a look as he slid his arm along the back of her seat, his hand came to rest on her shoulder. "It means relax."

She struggled to concentrate on what he was saying as his finger drew lazy circles on her upper arm. He turned toward her, his intense attention focused on her.

"I know what it means. I just didn't think you did," she said, knowing she was grasping at this conversation and trying to make something out of nothing. Anything to keep him from bringing up Lucinda again.

"Oh, honey, I know how to relax."

He was being sweet and she knew he'd deny it if she called him on it. Seeing this side of him made her believe that he could want her for more than six months. *This* was the man she could fall for, not the arrogant man who'd walked into her office this afternoon and told her that his mistresses wore what he provided.

She fingered the diamond choker at her neck. She was something he'd bought and paid for, like his fancy car with more gadgets than anything she owned. She was an accoutrement and she struggled to remember that he thought of her that way.

"Again with the lust thing."

The circles he was drawing on her arm got wider until the tip of his forefinger slipped under the strap of her dress, moving with slow sensual sweeps over her collarbone. "You're obsessed with making every conversation we have sexual."

No, she wasn't. She had just learned from dealing with men that they were easily led off topic when sex was introduced into the conversation. And hey, she was honest enough to admit that it was easier to resist him in the moonlight when she thought he was only after one thing.

"Isn't that what being a mistress is about?" she asked.

"I don't know. I suppose each woman has a different reason."

Somehow that made her feel a little better. "What about you? Why do you want a mistress?"

"My father was always happier with his mistresses than he was with my mother. I guess I just want to be happy. Does that make sense?"

"Yes," she said. More sense than she wanted it to.

Making Jeremy want more than six months with her was going to be harder than she'd first thought.

He left off caressing her arm and shoulder and traced the line of the choker. Her pulse sped up and the slow, steady rhythm of the music mirrored the beat of her heart.

She forgot about vindication and contracts. She forgot about wanting something that had been taken away from her too soon. She forgot about everything except the man sitting next to her.

The man filling her head with thoughts that she'd never had before. Thoughts of nighttime walks on the beach; thoughts of forever. The future had always been nebulous for her. As a young girl, the princess of her family, she'd awaited her future, sure that it would hold only more pampering and treasures. She'd never guessed that it could be such a harsh and cold place.

Despite what she might feel in this moment for Jeremy, she had to remember that the future wasn't a rosy, cheery place. The future, even one with him, would be filled with moments like the one she'd had tonight when she'd seen Lucinda. A moment that could make her stomach feel filled with lead.

"Don't think so much, honey."

"I can't help it."

"Yes, you can," he said, wrapping his arm around her and bending to kiss her. A sweet, gentle kiss….

Maybe the future wouldn't be so cold and harsh after all.

Jeremy's good intentions of relaxing Bella faded quickly when she melted in his arms. He held her loosely, trying to remember why he'd thought stopping at this very public spot would be a good idea.

He'd wanted to slow things down, to slow himself down and not rush his seduction. But at this moment, with her lips so tender under his, he couldn't recall why.

His cell phone rang again. Reluctantly he pulled away from Bella to glance at the caller ID. Kell. *Again.*

"I've got to take this."

She nodded and opened her door. "I'll give you some privacy."

He stopped her with his hand on her wrist. "Stay."

She sank back into the seat as he accepted the call.

"Kell, man, you know I'm on a date."

"I wanted to make sure you had all the information you needed."

"About?" he asked.

"Isabella."

He glanced over at the woman in question. She had her head tipped back against the headrest and her eyes closed. She tapped her fingers to the rhythm of the music playing. He had a sinking feeling in his gut that Kell wasn't calling to recommend Bella's event-planning company.

"And?"

Kell took a deep breath and Jeremy worried what his friend might have heard. "She's a gold digger, man. Lucinda remembers her. Don't be fooled by her designer gown or jewelry—she's penniless. And there's more you should know about her father."

Jeremy felt a twinge of guilt at the thought of his friends gossiping about them when they'd left. Talking about her gown and the jewelry that he'd insisted she wear. He had an inkling of understanding as to why Bella had blanched when she saw Lucinda. What had happened between those two?

"Thanks, I'll keep that in mind." Since they had a contractual arrangement, he wasn't too worried about any designs that Bella had on his money.

"You're still going to—"

"Do whatever I damn well please."

"It's your funeral."

"Thanks for the encouragement."

"Jeremy, I, uh, I just don't want to see you make the same mistake I did."

He knew that Kell didn't interfere unless he had a good reason. And Jeremy did appreciate his cousin looking out for him. Maybe he should set Kell straight on Bella. As soon as she wasn't sitting next to him. "Thanks, Kell. I won't. Are we still on for golf tomorrow?"

"Yeah," Kell said, and disconnected the call.

He tossed his phone into the center console and turned toward Bella. She opened her eyes and looked at him.

"Everything okay?" she asked, with a note of

caring in her voice that made him wonder yet again why she'd settle for a business relationship with him instead of a more personal one.

"Yes, fine."

"So what's next? Sorry about wigging out earlier. I'm not usually like that. You knocked me off balance by showing up out of the blue like you did."

He raised an eyebrow at her. "Glad to know that my plan worked."

She smiled. "You have a very devious mind."

"I'm a planner."

"Really? I'm more a reactor."

He had seen that firsthand. She seldom made plans for the long term. When he'd run into her three years ago, she'd been focused on getting Dare through college and hadn't thought beyond that. Even when making her business strategy, she seldom wanted to look more than six months ahead.

"I don't like to have to react. When you have a plan, you're in control."

She shook her head.

"You don't agree."

"Ah, sorry, but no. When you have a plan all you have is the illusion of control. You can't expect the unexpected."

"Like me coming to your office tonight."

"Exactly. I knew it was time to pay up, but thought I'd manage it from my end."

He'd meant to catch her off guard. When Bella

was prepared she was hard to read. She gave the scripted reactions to everything instead of letting him see a glimpse of the real woman. He'd only caught her by surprise twice, counting tonight. The first time, he'd kissed her—and offered to make her his mistress.

But then, her responses to him each time never failed to stagger him. He always built variables into his strategic plans for business and for his personal life, but she never responded the way he expected her to.

"We have two choices," he said.

"And they are?"

"We can still make our dinner reservation, or we can take a walk on the beach and then I'll take you home and cook for you."

"I'm not ready to be with other people right now," she said.

"Want to talk about it?"

"No. I'll deal with it."

"The way you always have," he said under his breath.

"What does that mean?"

"That you're too used to being on your own. I'm in your life now."

"For six months, Jeremy. When you're gone I'll be back where I started."

"I'm not gone yet."

"But you will be and I don't want to forget that."

"Until then I think we can have one hell of a ride, Bella."

She said nothing, and he wondered if this would be it. The moment when she decided that she'd had enough of him and his contract and walked away.

She sighed and put her hand on his thigh again. "I think I'd like for you to cook me dinner."

Four

Jeremy's house was plush and sophisticated. The trappings of his family's legacy of wealth were everywhere. It reminded her at once of her childhood home and she felt a pang in her heart as they walked by the pool in the back of the house.

The smell of hibiscus was thick in the air. The meal he'd prepared had been simple and delicious and she savored the novelty of having a man cook for her. He'd offered her an after-dinner drink but she declined. This wasn't the time to do too much drinking and the wine she'd had with dinner was giving her a sweet buzz.

She was a little sleepy, but wasn't ready for this

night to end. It had been a tumultuous ride, but she was getting used to that. It seemed everything with Jeremy was unexpected.

"What are you thinking of?" he asked, quietly coming up behind her.

She bit her lower lip. Honesty had been her policy since she'd realized that lying hurt her more than the truth.

"You."

"Hmm, that sounds good."

"Maybe."

"Maybe? That's all I get?"

"Yes. You're too arrogant for your own good," she said, but her words lacked heat. Tonight she'd seen a different side to him. A side that wasn't entirely unexpected. She'd been telling him the truth in the car—she was a reactor. But this situation was difficult for her. She wasn't sure how to react.

Inside she battled with her physical responses to him as a woman and what her mind was telling her. She needed to find a way to balance honesty with self-preservation. Because if she responded to him in the way she truly felt, she was so afraid she'd lose part of herself—her heart.

It would be so easy to melt into this role. To stop worrying about the future and just let the next six months bump along according to his design. But at the end of that six months what would she have left? The same things she had now…unless she planted the seeds of the future with Jeremy.

"You're thinking again."

She smiled at him and hoped her expression didn't reveal the sadness that was tingeing this moment.

"Sorry." She didn't say more than that, afraid that she'd blurt out more than she wanted him to know.

"Don't be. I do have some papers for you to go over. I've leased a luxury townhome for you to live in and I set up some accounts for you."

"I don't need any of that," she said. He'd already mentioned that he would provide housing and accounts, but the last thing she wanted was to take anything else from Jeremy. And she needed her real life. Her small home and her friends. They were what kept her grounded.

"I have certain standards."

"Just because I'm not in your financial tax bracket doesn't mean I live in a dump." To be fair, there was a time when it would have meant exactly that. But the last three years had been good to her and her business. She didn't live in the most prestigious neighborhood, like he did. But she lived in a nice area. A comfortable, middle-class neighborhood where people genuinely cared for each other, and not because of their social status or connections.

"I wasn't implying you lived in a dump."

Had she overreacted? She had no idea. Suddenly she wanted this night to end. She wanted to be back in her nice, safe little home, tucked under the quilt that used to grace her parents' bed, hidden away from the world so she could regroup.

"I can't put my life on hold for six months," she said, rubbing the back of her neck. This was the part she'd never been able to imagine when she'd thought of their contract. The part that made this temporary business arrangement all too real.

"I'm not asking you to." He brushed her hand aside and massaged the back of her neck and shoulders. His touch was just right, strong and firm.

Chills spread down her neck and arms. Her breasts felt fuller. Even though his touch wasn't sexual, she wanted it to be. She wanted more of the passion-filled kisses that had punctuated the last three years of her life.

"Relax, Bella. This is going to work out the way we both envision it," he said.

He slid his hands down her arms and drew her back against his body. His breath stirred the hair at the nape of her neck. She was completely surrounded by him and sank back against his tall, lean frame.

Why did he sound so reasonable? He was making her feel like she was being difficult, and that had never been her intention. She needed to be up front about what limitations she wanted on the relationship.

But she couldn't do it while she was in his arms.

Taking a deep breath, she stepped away from him, turning to face him. "I need to stay in my home. I'll be available for you on evenings and weekends. There will be some nights when I have to work, but I can come over here or even to that townhome if you want all of our sexual encounters to take place there."

"Sexual encounters."

"Aren't those the words you used in the contract we both signed?"

He closed the distance she'd put between them in one long stride. She couldn't help taking a step backward. Gone was the soft, tender lover. She couldn't really tell what he felt at this moment, but she suspected it was close to anger. She thought her blunt summation of their relationship might have been too baldly stated.

He'd let things get out of control in an effort to relax her and perhaps to make up for the encounter with Lucinda. But letting her boil down what was between them to nothing more than sexual encounters left a bad taste in his mouth, no matter that it was the truth.

From the very beginning the attraction between them had been electric. He couldn't explain it any other way. He knew that real sexual chemistry was rare. He had experienced it to lesser degrees with other women he'd dated, but from the first instant he'd seen her, his entire body had gone on high alert.

She'd been too thin and too tired to be interested in any advances he made, but she'd still responded. Responded and turned him down with regret because she had a teenage brother at home for whom she was responsible.

That had been part of the attraction, he admitted. Her total selflessness where her brother was concerned. He didn't have one acquaintance who would have done the same, except Kell. Kell would sacrifice himself for Jeremy, and Jeremy would do the same for his cousin.

But never for the women he'd been involved with. He'd thought perhaps that novel situation had been the driving factor in the attraction. He could have walked away from her—hell, who was he kidding? Walking away was never something he'd considered.

When he saw something he wanted, he went after it until he made it his own. And he was going to make her his. Completely his, no matter what she thought or how she tried to manage him and their time together. *Sexual encounters* was too tame a term to describe what he intended between them.

She bit her lower lip and he groaned out loud. Her mouth was full and lush and beckoned him like nothing else ever had.

He caught her hips in his hands and pulled her

toward him. Her eyes widened and she inhaled sharply but she didn't resist him.

"We're going to have more than sexual encounters, Bella."

"We are?"

"Yes," he said, lowering his head to hers. He dropped nibbling kisses along her brow and then slowly found her lips with his. All night long he'd kept a tight rein on his desire to devour her mouth. He knew how it tasted, always thought it couldn't be as lush and welcoming as he remembered. Yet it always was.

Her hands found his shoulders and she clung to him as he traced the seam of her lips with his tongue.

There had been something of a challenge in those words she'd uttered. And he didn't know if he would be able to prove her right or wrong. Part of him—the hard, hungry part of him—wanted sex. Craved the feel of her silky limbs against his.

There was a spark of wildness in her eyes that called to him. Her hands clasped his shoulders, making him feel like the strongest man in the world. He tilted his head to the side and plundered her mouth.

If she wanted this, then he'd be happy to oblige. He'd seduce her into his bed and use her until the passion between them ran its course and then send her on her way. She'd fulfill her promise to him and he'd have…he'd have Bella for a short time.

She tasted of some essence of woman that he was coming to associate only with her. She moaned deep in her throat as he thrust his tongue into her mouth. Her tongue stroked tentatively against his.

Sliding his hands down her back, he cupped her hips and pulled her more firmly against his body. He'd meant to keep the embrace light, but Bella made it too easy to forget his intentions.

He rubbed his growing erection against her and she made another soft sound in the back of her throat. Her nails dug into his shoulders through the layer of his shirt. She undulated against him.

He lifted his head. Her eyes were closed and her face was flushed with desire. He knew that it would take very little for him to persuade her to have sex with him, but with a few words she'd made him want her to admit there was more than sex between them.

He traced a path down the side of her neck to the choker he'd given her. He wanted to see her wearing just that and the moonlight. The image almost brought him to his knees.

He didn't know if she'd meant to remind him or herself with those words. Part of him wanted to just take what he needed. Show her how it would be if he really did just use her for sex.

But then her eyes opened and she looked at him and did something no woman had ever done before. Bella cupped his face and stood on tiptoe, touching her lips to his and whispering his name.

His heart beat too quickly in his chest and the lust that had taken control of his body abated as fear slowly crept through him. He wanted her more than he should.

· He let his hands fall away from her body and turned on his heel, heading back up to the house. Once inside, he went to the wet bar and mixed himself a drink.

How had the evening gotten so out of control? Bella stayed on the patio for a few extra minutes, trying to gather her senses and make some kind of plan to get safely out the door without throwing herself into Jeremy's arms.

His arms around her always felt so right. She shook her head, refusing to dwell on that. They needed to come to a compromise about their living arrangements for the next six months. She'd angered him with her summation of their relationship and she couldn't blame him.

Half the time she said things just to get a rise out of him. As she belatedly followed him into the house, she smiled to herself. She'd gotten more than one kind of rise out of him just now.

"What's so funny?"

"Oh, it was kind of an inside joke."

He waited, highball glass in one hand, hip cocked. He looked so virile and masculine standing there in the dim light provided by the wall sconces.

He took her breath away with the way he moved. And his contradictions. Why couldn't he have stuck to ordering her around?

She could resist Jeremy all day long when he was arrogant, but as soon as she felt his arms around her she was lost. Or was she found? She'd been lost for so long that she'd almost accepted it as the norm. But then he reminded her that there were still things she wanted in the world that had nothing to do with money, status or business success.

"You might not think it's funny."

"Try me," he said, knocking back his drink.

"Um…I was just thinking that I said what I did to get a rise out of you…"

He gave her a wry grin, but didn't move from the doorway.

"I'm sorry about what I said earlier. I should try to remember what Shelley advised."

"Your assistant?"

"She's more than just an employee, she's a friend."

"What did she say?"

"To enjoy you," she said.

"Tell me more."

She shook her head. "I don't want to talk about my friends," she said quietly, reluctant to reveal more than she had.

"Me either."

She took a few steps closer to him. They had to

come to some kind of compromise. "I kind of want to have things my way on everything."

"Yeah, I can understand that. I've been dealing with people for a long time. And I've learned that having everything in a contract is the only way to keep all sides from getting upset."

It sounded so cold, hearing him talk about sleeping with her the same way he'd approach a deal he brokered. Guard your heart, Bella, she thought. This man could hurt you.

"I've never been a mistress before. And I haven't experienced relationships the way you have. Most of the people I deal with are good on their word."

"What if they aren't?"

"Then I'm disappointed in them."

"With a contract there's no room for disappointment."

"Do you realize how cold that sounds?" she said before she could help herself. Her doubts were circling back to her.

He shrugged a shoulder and turned to the bar, pouring himself another mixed drink. "Can I get you something?"

She shook her head. She knew how Alice must have felt when she'd stumbled down the rabbit hole. Bella only wished there'd been a talking white rabbit to alert her that she was now in an alternate universe.

"Where are the papers you had for me to look at?"

"On the table," he said, gesturing with his glass toward the dining room.

The dining room was bigger than the master bedroom in her current house and recalled images of the one from her childhood. She remembered playing on hardwood floors just like this, sock-skating around the table while her mother sang in her beautiful contralto voice.

Oh, man. What was she doing here? No matter how many times she asked the question, she still hadn't found the answer she was looking for.

There was a manila file folder with her name written across it. She drew out a chair and sat down, opening the folder. Inside was an addendum to the contract she'd already signed. It listed the start and end dates for their relationship.

He had been thorough and very generous. The accounts he'd set up would last only as long as their relationship did, but the annuity he was providing for her for the six months would continue. He wouldn't be adding money into it, but by the terms and stipulations she read, he'd given her a cushion that would ensure she'd never again have to leave her house in the middle of the night one step ahead of the creditors.

She struck out the clause about the townhome, but left the accounts with the stipulation that they be paid from the annuity. She didn't want to take any more than was absolutely necessary. She changed the start and end dates by one day because she couldn't start tonight.

And hoped he'd understand. She added one addendum of her own and then initialed her changes and signed her name.

She glanced up to where he waited in the doorway and pushed the papers across the table toward him. "I made a few changes."

He walked into the room, glanced at the changes and initialed all of them, including the clause she'd added, without any questions. "I'll have my driver see you home. And I'll pick you up tomorrow night around eight."

"I'll be at an event. I'll send the address to your secretary in the morning."

He nodded. The emotionless set of his face and his dispassionate eyes made her feel cold. She stood, rubbing her hands up and down her arms.

He cursed under his breath, closing the distance between them in two long strides. He pulled her into his arms and kissed her. Not a tentative meeting of the mouths, but the kind of kiss that went beyond the barriers of two people attracted to each other and straight to the souls of two lonely people.

In his kiss she felt a desperation that echoed what was inside her. She wrapped her arms around his waist and held on to him like she'd never let go. Only she knew, deep inside, that she never wanted to.

Five

Jeremy checked his watch for the second time, realizing that Bella was late. He got out of his car, leaving the keys with the valet, and entered the Norton Museum of Art in West Palm Beach.

"Sorry," Bella said, hurrying over to him. She wore a blue crepe dress that ended just above her knees and she had her hair pulled back in a professional-looking twist. She smiled at him but he could tell she was harried.

"Is something wrong?"

"Just horribly short-staffed. I'm going to be at least forty-five more minutes. If you want to go ahead to the restaurant I can meet you at the bar there."

Drinking alone had never appealed to him. Especially when Bella waited somewhere else. Thoughts of her had crept into his mind throughout the day until Daniel had text-messaged him to get his head in the game. It was the first time he could recall a woman interfering with his business and he didn't like it.

"No."

She put her hand on his wrist. Her slim, cool fingers rested right above the Swiss Army watch that his dad had given him. The watch was a constant reminder of his old man.

"I really can't leave right now, Jeremy."

He twisted his hand around to capture hers, rubbing his thumb over the back of her knuckles. "I'll come with you. Putting out fires is my specialty."

She didn't pull her hand free as she led the way back down the hallway to the theater room in the museum.

"It is? You don't look like a firefighter."

"Well, there's more than one kind of fire."

"I know that," she said under her breath.

"Are you feeling a few flames?"

"Don't even start. Twice today I—"

He pulled them to a stop in the doorway leading toward the service corridor when she didn't go on. "What?"

She shook her head. "I really need to go back to the ballroom."

"Then tell me what you were going to say."

She nibbled on her lower lip, a gesture that never failed to make him want to kiss her.

"Just that twice today I called one of our staffers by your name."

"Does he look like me?"

"Not at all. I was just—" She pulled away from him. "Don't let this go to your head, but you were on my mind."

How could he not? He tugged her back toward the main hallway. "Let's get your problems solved so we can go somewhere private. Then you can tell me all the details."

"I don't need you to solve my problems."

"I know that. It's just that I'm rather effective at it."

"Really? What's the most effective way?" she asked, tipping her head to the side in a flirtatious gesture. "I've never had a billionaire businessman give me advice on managing my workforce before."

"Keep being sassy and you still won't."

"Sassy?"

"Sassy."

"Hmm…no one's ever called me that before. Is that the key to keeping the staff in line?"

"Intimidation is. You scare the bejeezus out of your staff and then they work more efficiently."

She laughed, just like he hoped she would. "I'm not very intimidating."

"Have you ever tried to be?" he asked. He

doubted she had. There was an innate goodness that surrounded Bella. He suspected that was part of what had originally drawn him to her. Despite the fact that she'd been down on her luck, she'd still been looking out for those around her instead of just focusing on herself.

"Well, no. That's not my style, really. Even when Dare was rebelling and I knew I should be tough on him, I couldn't." In her voice he heard the echoes of what he'd heard that night three years ago when they'd struck their deal. Her doubts in herself and her abilities to pull her brother back from the edge.

He let go of her hand, sliding his arm around her waist and drawing her into his side. She held her body stiff until he stroked his free hand down her spine. Then she relaxed against him.

"He respects you," she said quietly.

"He admires you," Jeremy said. He didn't know how he'd become a father-confessor to Dare McNamara, but somehow he had. The young man e-mailed him a couple times a week and called every few days to check in.

Jeremy knew part of it was that Dare expected him to keep an eye on Isabella. Her brother wanted to make sure she was looked after. And as Dare said, he wasn't man enough to do it yet.

Since taking care of Bella played into his plans, that was an easy enough promise to give Dare. Sometimes he had a few qualms about how Dare would feel if he knew the nature of the relationship between him and Bella, but that was no one else's business.

"I really don't have time to be talking about my brother or leaning on you."

"What do we need to do?"

"The florist dumped the arrangements in the kitchen and I need someone to place one on each round table."

"Um…"

"Come on, Jeremy. It'll be good for you. It'll build character and earn you my gratitude."

"That's all well and good but I want more than gratitude."

"Help me out and I'll give you whatever you ask for."

"Deal," he said, holding open the door to the convention space and entering Bella's world. He watched her direct her staff and realized he respected the way she worked. She didn't micromanage anyone—just expected them to do the job they'd been assigned. And he noticed that everyone worked harder when she was around them. Not because they were afraid of her, he suspected, but to bask in the glow of her smile and the praise that accompanied it.

He told himself he wasn't the same as these workers. That he was here to collect the woman who was contractually bound to him. But when she glanced at the finished tables and smiled at him, he felt something stir inside him.

Something that had nothing to do with lust. Something that wasn't bound by a contract. Something he hoped like hell was going to go away when his time with Bella was up.

"I'm so glad you're here," she said.

He walked away without saying a word because he wasn't too sure that *he* was happy. He'd wanted Bella and gone after her with the single-minded determination he went after anything he wanted, and was only now realizing that getting her might not be his smartest business decision.

She'd expected Jeremy to whisk her out of the museum and to a private place where they'd be intimate. But when the bar association members started to arrive, some acquaintances of his were in the group. He signaled her to join him but she shook her head and motioned that she'd be a few minutes.

Every time she was in his presence he knocked her a little further off-kilter. She pulled her cell phone from her pocket to check the time and pretend she was busy instead of going to his side. She wasn't ready to be at his side. Not now. She needed a reality check. The kind that focusing on the details of her job could deliver.

"There you are," Shelley said, coming up behind her. She had a clipboard in one hand and a radio in the other. She looked like a staffer, unlike Bella, who was dressed for her date with Jeremy. She realized that she was right where she'd never wanted to be. Right on the cusp of two worlds. Her two worlds.

Her two lives. The one she'd once had and dreamed of getting back. And this one, the one she'd built from the wreckage.

"Please don't give me bad news," she said when Shelley reached her side.

The blonde had her hair pulled back in a ponytail and her button-down, oxford shirt open at the collar. She looked young but competent. "Geez. Is that my rep now?"

"Well you did keep coming to find me with another challenge to report."

"Challenge...I like that. I'm going to use it the next time my boyfriend says I'm too much work."

Shelley was a dear, sweet person who didn't have a mean bone in her body. And her boyfriend took advantage of that. "Did you need something?"

"Yes. I'm playing delivery girl again." She reached into her pocket and pulled out a small envelope. One that the florist had inadvertently put in the arrangements. That had been one of the first challenges of the day—removing all those picks with the blank cards in them.

Her name was written across the back of the cream-colored envelope. "Thanks, Shelley."

"No problem. He's very romantic."

Bella had no idea how to respond to that. "We need to double-check the jackets on the waitstaff. I don't want anyone going out there with stains."

"I'll double-check. You need to leave."

"Are you sure?" she asked. Her duty manager had been involved in a car accident, so there was no senior person at the event. Bella had toyed with canceling on Jeremy, but Shelley had made a bid to be in charge, wanting to use this event to prove herself.

Shelley rolled her eyes. "Yes."

"You've got my cell number, right?"

Shelley shook her head, reached over and took the museum radio from her hand. "You're being challenging."

Bella laughed. "You're right. Sorry about that. I'll see you in the morning."

"Have fun tonight," Shelley said as she walked away.

Bella left the theater and went in the back to collect her purse. She'd left her car at the office since Jeremy had said he'd pick her up.

She lifted the back flap and stared down at the card inside. She pulled it out. It was a cheap generic one, the kind that florists used for bulk arrangements.

On it was simply a phone number. This was what Shelley had thought was romantic?

What had she expected? Some kind of love note?

She was his mistress, not a woman he was seducing. She was a sure thing. And she was beginning to realize she had absolutely no idea how to convince him she should be more than a mistress.

She dialed it, a little disappointed. And mad at herself for being upset. She had no claims to Jeremy other than those he'd laid out in writing. Why had she forgotten that?

"Harper."

"It's Bella," she said, moving away from the convention food and beverage staff, who were making a lot of noise as they readied all the dishes to go out to the tables at one time.

"Are you free now?" he asked.

"Yes. I'm all yours."

"Mine? Not quite."

"What do you mean?"

"Why didn't you join me earlier?"

"I had some stuff to finish up."

"Stuff? That sounds like an excuse. You're my mistress, Bella. That means that when we are together—"

"I'm working tonight, Jeremy. That's my first priority."

"Why?"

"Why what?" she asked, stalling. She really had to figure out how to filter every thought that came into her head so that they didn't all end up coming out of her mouth.

"Are we going to play this kind of game?"

"You started it," she said.

She hated that he'd called her on avoiding him. She was nervous again, and that was beginning to bother her. Why hadn't she figured him out yet? Normally it took her maybe two meetings with a person to decide how to deal with them. But with him…

She sighed. "I'm sorry. I was being sarcastic and it was uncalled for."

"Bella, what am I going to do with you?"

"Anything your contract gives you the right to."

He said nothing for a long moment and she heard the head of the Palm Beach Bar Association get up and start talking.

"I'll meet you in the Tsai atrium and we can start our night."

"Okay."

She hung up before he had a chance to say anything else. No more nerves. She'd promised herself that this morning. She wanted more from Jeremy than six months and she wasn't going to get that by hiding.

Seeing her tonight with her staff and the way she'd treated him when they were with other people showed him that she was still nervous about any intimacy between them. And he knew the quickest way to push past it was through seduction.

He had been to many events at the Norton during his lifetime and knew the museum like the back of his hand. He'd attended most of the events with one of his parents. Never the two of them together. They were happier apart, something his father had explained to Jeremy when he'd turned nine.

That talk about marriage and relationships had been diverted by a few innocent questions about sex. Because nine-year-old Jeremy hadn't been too sure that Kell had known what he was talking about when he said that a boy's penis had to get hard before he could have sex.

The sex part…well, his dad had firm opinions about it. He'd said that women saw sex as more than just a physical release. That a gentleman didn't marry for sex, he had mistresses for sex. And that when a man found the right woman, sex was an incredible thing.

Bella stood in the center of the now empty atrium on the cracked ice terrazzo floor. Remembering his father's advice about women and sex made him realize that he wanted Bella to be different. To somehow be the kind of woman that Lucinda must be for Daniel to still be so into her.

But he was afraid to take the risk of caring for her. He would likely only confirm that he was essentially his father's son. After all, he was definitely his father's progeny in the business world. Making money and turning a profit was something that came easily to him. As did the women…and there had never been anyone he wanted to marry.

And now, there Bella stood, her dress so close to the same deep blue as the tiles that she looked like part of the decor. An ethereal woman that he could only glimpse. He hated that. For most of his life he'd struggled with trying to hold on to people in his life. He didn't have a lot of lasting relationships.

The heels of his Italian loafers made a soft sound as he approached and she pivoted to face him. He hesitated there, unable to move toward her. Feeling once again that punch in the gut. She was more beautiful than any woman he'd ever seen.

He walked up to her and had to fight the urge to put his arms around her. She was a mistress. His mistress. *His.*

That word resonated inside him. He knew it wasn't politically correct but it suited him to claim her even if only in his own mind. There was something soothing about knowing exactly what to expect from another person.

She turned to look at him. "I love this place. It's so soothing and quiet at night."

"Then you're going to love the surprise I have planned for you."

"Love it?"

There was skepticism in her voice, but he wasn't daunted. Now that he had a plan, he was back on his game. Seduction was the key to wooing her and having her.

"Wait and see."

He took her hand in his and led her to a small, wedge-shaped room off the atrium. The J. Ira and Nick Harris Family Pavilion. There was a small table set in the middle of the room in front of the glass doors that led to the Italian gardens outside.

But it was the ceiling that made the room. The Chihuly glass was spectacular and Jeremy knew he'd made the right decision when he heard her breath catch.

Her hand fell away from his and she walked farther into the room. The lighting behind the Chihuly ceiling painted the room in hues of aquatic blues and greens.

"Jeremy…this is lovely. Are we having dinner here?"

"Yes," he said, crossing to the freestanding ice-bucket to pour them both a glass of champagne.

"This is…okay, I do love it."

"What did I tell you?"

"You're doing the arrogance thing again."

"In this case I think I've earned the right."

"Okay, I'll give you that."

He handed her the champagne flute and then tipped his glass to hers. "To the next six months."

She nodded and took a delicate sip of her drink, keeping eye contact with him the entire time. But he saw her hand tremble as she lifted the glass to her lips.

She put her glass on the table and walked slowly around the room, observing the ceiling from every angle. When she came back to the table, he signaled to the waitstaff to begin serving their meal.

He held her chair, seating her. When he pulled his own chair out he saw the small gift box he'd asked to be put there.

He picked it up and placed it on the table.

She glanced at the gift box and then back up at him. He couldn't read the expression in her usually expressive eyes.

"You don't have to seduce me," she said carefully.

"That's my privilege."

"Oh."

"Yes, oh." He handed her the package and watched as she held it carefully between her fingers.

"I'd rather you make a donation to charity than keep giving me gifts."

He shook his head. "Mistresses should take as many gifts from their lovers as possible."

He'd hurt her. He could see it in the way she subtly flinched and sank back in her chair. She let the small present fall to the table.

He felt like an ass. He'd been on his game just a few moments earlier. Why had he said that? It shouldn't matter to him if she didn't want his gifts—and yet it did. She was already blurring the lines between mistress and…girlfriend.

"Just open the present, Bella."

She removed the ribbon and the wrapping and then opened the box. Inside was a small placard that showed a Chihuly sculpture he'd ordered for her. It would be delivered in three weeks time.

"Thank you, Jeremy."

He shrugged like it meant nothing to him, but it was too late to pretend with himself. His gut-deep confirmation earlier that she was his made that impossible. He could only fall back on the contract they had between them. Hope that six months of holding her would be enough.

After they ate, he took her on a moonlit stroll through the Renaissance-inspired gardens and then led the way back to his car.

She'd relaxed during the walk but his tension had increased. He wanted her. And that seemed more dangerous now then it had at the beginning of the evening when he'd felt safe and protected by his contract. He could have everything he wanted from her. But now he knew that their arrangement wasn't going to protect him from the emotions that she brought swirling to the surface.

Six

Bella had no idea where they were going as they flew down the highway. The top was down on Jeremy's convertible and the breeze made it impossible to talk, which was something of a relief.

Tonight had made her feel every inch the pampered woman of a wealthy man. There was something very attractive to her about being Jeremy's mistress. The problem was that the glimpses she'd seen of the possessive man Jeremy was made her want him for more than a temporary affair.

She hoped they weren't headed for the town house he'd leased. Suddenly, she thought of it as a test for him. If he took her to the townhome, then she'd know she hadn't made any progress in getting him to see her as more than a mistress. But it wouldn't make it any easier for her to remember that this was an arrangement and not a real love affair.

But damn it all, it was starting to feel that way. He should have just taken her to dinner instead of going out of his way to have a meal catered for them. And she knew the Norton's convention policy—they had minimums like everyone else. He must have spent a fortune on dinner.

Money wasn't an issue for Jeremy. She should have remembered that. Maybe the evening was nothing more than a convenience. Maybe what she'd interpreted as a romantic gesture was just the way he operated.

She didn't think so. The Chihuly glass sculpture was breathtaking, even in a picture. She wanted to take the card out of her purse and look at it again. But she didn't.

As they neared town, she glanced over at him. His attention stayed focused on the road and she noticed that he handled the car with ease. Not surprising. He did everything with ease.

He slowed even further and pulled into the parking lot of the Palm Beach hotel. The hotel was old and refined, a grande dame in the area. It was known for luxury and quality.

Please don't let this be where he is taking me, she

thought. She didn't want the first time they made love to be in a hotel. She wanted it to be in a place that meant something to one of them.

As he neared the valet parking station, she reached over and put her hand on his thigh. "What are we doing here?"

"Meeting some business associates for a drink."

More time spent waiting. The tension that had been riding her for the last two days—heck, to be honest, the last three years—tightened painfully inside her. She knew that Daniel Posner was his business partner. And Lucinda Cannon was Daniel's wife. She wasn't ready for another meeting with either of them.

She didn't want to add another nerve-inducing element to the evening, and talking to his business associates wasn't going to relax her. But she'd never say that to him. She owed him. He'd spent an insane amount of money on her already and she hadn't done anything other than kiss him.

"Is that okay?" he asked, looking pointedly down at his leg.

She was digging her nails into his thigh. "Of course."

She hastily removed her hand, putting it back in her lap. Oh, my God, this was getting out of control. Why had she ever thought she could do this? Because she'd been desperate. And desperation was the creator of opportunity.

It didn't feel like opportunity right now, as she looked at the beautiful hotel entrance. A place where she'd once attended cotillion dances and afternoon teas with her mother's circle of friends. She'd taken tennis lessons from a Wimbledon champion at this hotel. And played golf with her father a lifetime ago.

"Who are we meeting?"

"My partner and his wife, plus a very important client, and his wife."

"Daniel?"

"Yes. Is that a problem?" he asked.

She shrugged, determined to play it cool this evening. She refused to give Lucinda the power of unnerving her, though her sweaty palms said the other woman already had done so.

"Not at all. Who's the client?" she asked. This might be the perfect opportunity for her to show him that she'd make a better wife than mistress. The kind of woman he'd want by his side in business and pleasure.

"Frederick Merriweather. We've been trying to convince him to merge with our company."

"And tonight is another attempt?"

Jeremy pulled the car to the side of the driveway and stopped. "Yes, it is. I'm glad to see that you're so interested in this meeting."

"Why?"

He shrugged.

She waited. But he didn't say anything else. She started to feel small and insignificant. And very much, she realized, like a mistress.

She turned her head away from him. She didn't want to play games. Games were their own form of lying. And she had played enough of them when her mom was alive.

Let's pretend we don't see the Cannons or the Fell-Murrays or anyone else we used to know.

"Just tell me why, Jeremy."

He reached across the space in the car, fingers on her cheek. "Because it's the first interest you've shown in something for me."

Didn't he realize she paid attention to every detail that was his life? It was probably a good thing that he didn't, at least not yet. But she took as a good sign that he wanted her attention. "Then tell me what you need me to do. I'm pretty good at putting people at ease."

"Just be yourself," he said.

He cupped his fingers around the back of her head and drew her steadily toward him. In his eyes she saw the light of something more than desire.

It made her want to trust him, she thought. But then his head bent toward hers and everything in her body tensed in awareness and need. Her blood flowed heavier in her veins. Her breasts felt fuller and her lips tingled. She started to close her eyes but then kept them open.

She wanted to know how he felt when he kissed her. Did he reveal anything? She noticed the tiny gold flecks in his light green-gray eyes. She noticed the way his pupils had dilated and his nostrils flared right before she felt his mouth on hers.

She closed her eyes then. It was impossible to think of anything other than Jeremy when his mouth touched hers. The details of their deal dropped away as she created new memories of this man.

Of the way his hands moved over her skin like he was trying to learn her by feel. The way his tongue conquered her mouth with languid thrusts as if he had all night to learn the taste of it. The way he rubbed his thumb over her moist lips and then held her hand as he drove to the entrance of the hotel.

When he put his hand low on her back and escorted her into the hotel, she no longer felt like an outsider.

The bar was crowded, but Jeremy found Daniel and Frederick with no trouble. He wanted this meeting to go smoothly and quickly so he could hustle Bella home. And then take her to bed. He'd set up the meeting to put Bella more at ease in his world, part of his deal with her.

But his body was tight and his mind was only on the woman at his side, not the upcoming meeting. He'd been a little rattled when she'd asked him what he needed of her. He didn't want to analyze it, yet the words kept circling around in his head. He needed her there because the other men would have their wives and it would keep the party even.

There was a sense of rightness in having her by his side. But he knew that it was a mistake to feel possessive about her. He wasn't a man who kept things. He prided himself on looking to the future. On moving through life unencumbered.

Bella was just one more pleasure to be enjoyed as he moved forward. Once he had her silky body under his and he claimed her, had her, he could move on.

That elusive thing about her would be realized and she'd become like every other woman he'd had a relationship with. Just another mistress.

Frederick was an older man in his late forties with a leonine mane of blond hair that made him look like an aging hippie. He wore a Brooks Brothers suit and a pinky ring. Frederick was a self-made man who didn't care what anyone thought about the way he and his wife dressed.

"Evening, Frederick. Where's Mary?"

"She saw something in the window of the boutique that she had to have. Who is this?"

"Bella McNamara. Bella, this is Frederick Merriweather."

"It's nice to meet you, Frederick," Bella said.

Jeremy nodded toward Daniel. "And I'm sure you remember my partner, Daniel Posner."

"Yes. Good to see you again, Daniel."

They shook hands and then Jeremy seated Bella at the table.

"You'll have to go to the bar if you want a drink," Daniel said.

"What would you like?" he asked Bella.

"Drambuie, please," she said.

He made his way to the bar to get their drinks.

"She doesn't look the way she used to."

Jeremy glanced over to see Lucinda standing next to him. Lucinda was one of the most beautiful women he'd ever met. She had classically good looks and she'd been raised in a moneyed world that showed in every graceful movement she made.

His family had socialized with hers, but he'd never noticed her as a child or teenager. In fact, until Daniel had started dating her, he'd never paid much attention to her.

"What did she look like?"

"At fourteen?"

He nodded. God, he hadn't realized how young she'd been when her world had fallen apart.

"More like me. Manicured, pedicured and hair chemically perfect."

He smiled at the faint mocking tone in Lucinda's voice. "Circumstances change."

"Yes, they do," Lucinda said.

"What are you trying to tell me?"

"I'm not sure. Her family and mine were once very close…"

Jeremy had done some Internet research on Bella and had read the AP newswire accounts of her father's fall and consequent suicide. And then just a tiny article when her mother died a few short years later. But there were details of her life that he couldn't fill in. How did a girl who was a princess turn into the single-mother type she'd been when he met her? True, it was her brother she'd been raising, but…

"When did you lose touch?" he asked, prying the way he would if this were a business deal. He'd never expected to glean information from Lucinda, whom he thought of usually as someone to be avoided since she was always trying to foist her single friends on him.

She shrugged and bit her lower lip. "When she stopped moving in our circle. She's not like us anymore, Jeremy."

He wasn't sure where she was going with this conversation, but had an inkling of why Bella had been so upset when she'd seen Lucinda the other night.

"Just spit it out. I'm not good at guessing games."

"No, you're not. That's why you need Daniel."

"In business I do need him and the subtle way he has of smoothing over my rough edges, but that still doesn't tell me about Bella and you."

"When she lost everything, she became a different person. She wasn't the girl she used to be, and to be honest I'm not sure that she isn't dating you for some kind of revenge."

"I don't understand."

"She means I wasn't suitable to speak to any longer."

He hadn't heard Bella come up to them. Lucinda shrugged delicately and stepped away from them. She stopped a few steps away to look back at Bella, and there was tension between the women that went beyond not talking to one another.

"Well, you and I both know that we don't socialize with the staff."

Bella froze. He wrapped his arm around her shoulder and pulled her solidly against him. She put her hand on his lapel and he felt the fine tremors in her body.

"Bella's not the staff any longer, Lucinda."

"Of course she isn't. She's your…what exactly is she, Jeremy?"

Bella cleared her throat and he saw a flash of her temper. That same temper that she always tried to hide. "None of your business, Lucinda. We're not friends any longer."

"And whose fault is that?"

"Assigning blame is a juvenile thing to do," Bella said in a small voice.

He had the feeling that there was much more between the two women than a change in Bella's financial circumstances. And though he was curious, he knew it was past time to put an end to this.

"We need to get back to the table. We're here for a business meeting."

"Of course," Lucinda said and made her way to Daniel's side.

He handed Bella her Drambuie. "Want to talk about it?"

She shook her head.

He couldn't stand the hurt in her eyes and wanted to do whatever he could to soothe it—to soothe her. "Bella—"

"Leave it, Jeremy. I'm not your girlfriend. I'm your mistress."

Her words struck him like a barb. And this was why he didn't want to allow her any closer than he had to.

"That's right. You are."

They didn't talk much on the car ride back to his place and Bella was glad of it. She had no idea how to make amends for her stupid comments. Once again she'd allowed Lucinda to get the better of her and to threaten a relationship that was coming to mean a lot to her.

She needed to apologize to Jeremy. Wanted to get the tension between them out of the way before they were intimate. And she knew without a shadow of a doubt that Jeremy was going to take her to his bed tonight. If for no other reason than to prove to them both that she was nothing more than his mistress.

She swallowed hard, searching for some words. Any words. *I'm sorry* wouldn't do, because then she'd have to admit that she realized she'd hurt his feelings earlier.

But once they entered his house, she was nervous about more than the apology, which was so silly because she wanted Jeremy. Her lips still tingled from his kiss in the car earlier.

Maybe that had played a part in her remarks to him. She had a history of shooting herself in the foot socially when she was…

"Jeremy?"

"Yes." He tossed his keys on the table in the hallway leading from the garage to the house. Standing on the threshold of the media room, he didn't turn to look at her.

"I…" She just couldn't say it. Didn't want to have to talk about Lucinda and the bad blood between them. Lucinda hadn't been particularly nice to her, but Bella knew she hadn't been all that good to Lucinda, either.

"You?" He pivoted on his heel.

She took a deep breath. "You know I've said that you're arrogant."

He nodded.

"Well, I'm not. When I'm unsure of myself—

and it happens more than I like to admit—I lash out. It's my way of protecting myself."

He leaned against the wall, crossing his arms over his chest.

"When did you start doing that?" he asked.

She took a deep breath. "Probably the summer I was fifteen and my mother started working for the Cannons as their upstairs maid. I helped her sometimes. It was awkward. I…I've never been able to just be quiet and pretend nothing bothers me."

"So you attack?"

"Yes."

He nodded. "Was there anything else?"

She shook her head.

"Then let's go have another drink before we head upstairs."

"Jeremy."

"What?"

"I don't like this tension between us. Despite everything, we've always been friendly. Let me do something to make it up to you."

He rubbed the back of his neck, and she realized that tonight might really be a sexual encounter. And she'd have to renege on her word.

She didn't give herself easily and had slept with only one other man. An event which was singularly unmemorable. She wanted earth-shattering passion with Jeremy, but a big part of her believed that was just the stuff of romantic stories—that in real life, sex was just sweaty and somewhat enjoyable.

"Come inside and we can discuss this," he said.

She followed him into the media room. He shrugged out of his jacket, tossing it over the back of the couch.

"I really enjoyed meeting Frederick and Mary," she said. As soon as they'd returned to the group, she'd realized her faux pas with Jeremy and had tried to make up for it by charming his would-be business associate.

She didn't know why she was talking about the business meeting he'd had. She certainly didn't want to open up the conversation to Lucinda. God knows she didn't want to think about the way she'd felt when she saw the two of them talking at the bar. A part of her knew that there was nothing Lucinda could say that Jeremy didn't already know. He'd seen her at rock-bottom.

"They liked you, too. I'm having a party on my yacht for them on Saturday."

She was grateful for the subject change.

"Do you want to use my caterer?" she asked, trying to ignore the fact that he'd removed his tie and loosened the top two buttons of his shirt.

"No. I want you by my side and not thinking about business."

"Oh," she said, feeling a little hurt. "I'm really the best event planner in the area."

"I don't doubt that."

"Then why don't you want me to take care of the details? It's short notice but I can—"

"Bella."

"Yes?"

"I have a personal chef who'll attend to the details, and if it's really so important to you, you can make the menu choices."

"Okay. I can hire servers for you, too."

"Forget about business. You have only one thing to think about right now."

"And that is?"

"Being my mistress," he said, and took her in his arms.

He tipped her head back and she met his gaze. He was serious now. And she realized she was seeing the real man. The trappings of society were stripped away as he watched her.

He wanted her.

She shivered. No man had ever wanted her this much. She was acutely aware of her femininity and the primitive power that she carried with it.

She caressed his back, felt the power in his shoulders. His arms shifted around her. One around her waist, the other low on her hips.

He didn't speak, didn't have to. At this moment words would be superfluous and neither of them needed to talk about anything.

His hair was cool and silky under her fingers.

She cupped his head in both of her hands, standing on her tiptoes as she drew his head down to hers.

She pressed her lips to his and traced the seam between them with her tongue. He tasted faintly of the scotch he'd consumed at the hotel and something else that she associated only with Jeremy.

He groaned deep in his throat, shifting her in his arms, lifting her off her feet. His mouth never left hers as he carried her up the stairs to his bedroom.

Seven

He set her on her feet next to his bed. The bed-room had one wall that was all windows. Framed in glass Bella saw the stars and the subtle lighting around the pool.

At this moment she was so very afraid that Jeremy would think she was only here because of the contract. And yet, at the same time, it would make things so much easier if that's what he believed.

Liar.

She grimaced. No matter how many times she said the words, they weren't true. She was here with Jeremy because she wanted the man and he'd…he'd gone to a lot of trouble for her. She was touched in a way that she didn't want to be.

He looked at her through half-lidded eyes, making her hyperaware of him and at the same time of her own body. She felt his gaze moving over her. She shifted her legs and let her arms drop to her sides.

She didn't need to protect herself from the past tonight. She was here with Jeremy. The man she'd been thinking about too much of the time. And damned if she wasn't going to enjoy him.

"Still want to talk about my party on Saturday?"

She bit her lip to keep from laughing. He was too confident, too sure of himself and with plenty of cause. He reached for her and pulled her into his arms. He lowered his head and she held her breath.

Brushing his lips over her cheek, he held her close but with a tenderness no man had shown her before. His long fingers caressed her neck, slow sweeps up and down until she shivered in his arms. She needed more from him. She grabbed his shoulders, tipped her head and opened her mouth under his.

He sighed her name as she thrust her tongue into his mouth. Sliding his arms down her back, he edged her toward the bed. It hit the backs of her legs and she sat down. He followed her, never breaking their kiss.

His tongue moved on hers with ease, tempting her further, tasting her deeper and making her long for him. Her skin felt too tight. Her breasts were heavy, craving his touch. Between her legs she was moistening for him, ready for him.

Squirming, she shifted around until she was on his lap, her legs straddling him. She lifted her head to look down at him. His skin was flushed, his lips wet from her kisses. She flexed her fingers against his shoulders.

God, he really was solid muscle.

"Take your shirt off," she said. She'd been longing to touch his chest since that long-ago summer day when she'd served him at the yacht club.

He reached between them, the backs of his fingers brushing her breasts as he unbuttoned his shirt. She shook from the brief contact and bit her lip to keep from asking for more.

He unbuttoned the small pearl buttons that held the bodice of her dress. Ran his finger down the center of her body, over her sternum and between her ribs. Lingered on her belly button and then stopped at the waistband of her high-cut thong panties.

He slowly traced the same path upward again. This time his fingers feathered under the demi-cups of her ice-blue bra, barely touching her nipples. Both beaded, and a shaft of desire pierced Bella, shaking her.

She needed more. She wanted more. Her heart beat so swiftly and loudly she was sure he could hear it. She scraped her fingernails lightly down his chest. He groaned, the sound rumbling up from his chest. He leaned back, bracing himself on his elbows.

And let her explore. This was so different from the hurried couplings she'd had with that one boyfriend in the past. Encounters that had happened in the dark and were over almost before they'd begun.

His muscles jumped under her touch. She circled his nipple but didn't touch it. Scraped her nail down the center line of his body, following the fine dusting of hair that narrowed and disappeared into the waistband of his pants.

His stomach was rock-hard and rippled when he sat up. He reached around her back and unhooked her bra and then pushed the cups up out of his way. He pulled her closer until the tips of her breasts brushed his chest.

"Bella." He said her name like a prayer.

His hard-on nudged her center and she shifted on him, trying to find a better touch, but it was impossible with the layers of cloth between them. Her dress was hiked up but it wasn't enough.

He kissed his way down her neck and bit lightly at her nape. She shuddered, clutching at his shoulders, grinding her body harder against him.

He pulled the fabric of her dress up to her waist, slipping his hands under the cloth. Those big hands burned hot on her skin as he cupped her butt and urged her to ride him faster, guiding her motions against him. He bent his head and his tongue stroked her nipple.

Everything in her body clenched. She clutched at Jeremy's shoulders as her climax washed over her. She collapsed against his chest, and he held her close. Bella hugged him to her and closed her eyes, reminding herself that to Jeremy this was just an agreement. But it didn't change the fact that she felt like she'd just found the man she'd been secretly dreaming of.

Jeremy had never seen anything more beautiful than the woman in his arms. She was so responsive to his touch and he wanted more. It fed his obsession in a way he hadn't expected. If he didn't take her soon he was going to self-combust.

The word *mine* swirled around in his head.

She pushed his shirt off his shoulders and he tugged it off, tossing it away. She shrugged out of her dress and bra. She was exquisitely built, soft, feminine. Her breasts were full and her skin flushed from her recent orgasm.

He ran his hands slowly over her torso, almost afraid to believe that after all these years, after all his negotiating, she was really here. Finally, in his bed, where he'd been fantasizing about her for so long.

Her nipples were tight little buds beckoning his mouth. He'd barely explored her before and he needed to now. He needed to find out how she reacted to his every touch.

He fingered her nipples carefully and she shifted her shoulders, trying to increase the pressure of his touch. "Tell me what you want."

"Don't you know?" she asked, her hands coming to his wrists, trying to control his movements.

He shook his head. "I want the words, Bella."

"I want…" she blurted.

He realized then that there was something very fragile inside this ultracompetent and professional woman. He pulled her more fully into his arms. Cradled her to his chest. She closed her eyes and buried her face in his neck. Each exhale went through him. God, he wanted her.

He was so hard and hot for her that he could come in his pants. But he was going to wait. He felt the minute touches of her tongue against his neck. Her hand slid down his chest and opened his belt, unfastening the button at his waistband and then lowering his zipper.

Hot damn.

Her hand slid inside his pants and his boxers. Smoothly her touch traveled up and down his length. He tightened his hands on her back. He glanced down his body to watch her working him with such tender care and he had to grit his teeth not to end it all right then. But he wanted to be inside her the next time one of them climaxed.

She smiled up at him. *Little minx.*

"I want you, Jeremy. All of you, deep inside me."

"You're going to have me," he said, his voice raspy.

She pushed the rest of her clothing away. His breath caught in his throat. She was exactly as he'd dreamed she'd be. Nipped-in waist, long slender legs and full breasts. He nudged her over on her back.

He leaned down, capturing her mouth with his as he shoved his pants farther down his legs. She opened her legs and he settled between her thighs.

The humid warmth of her center scorched his already aroused flesh. He thrust against her without thought. Damn, she felt good.

He wanted to enter her totally naked. At least this first time. But that was a huge risk and one he knew better than to take.

He pushed away from her, fumbled with his pants, taking them all the way off along with his boxers, then found the condom he'd put in the pocket earlier today.

He glanced over at her and saw that she was watching him. The fire in her eyes made his entire body tighten with anticipation. He put the condom on one-handed and turned back to her.

"Hurry."

"Not a chance. I'm going to savor you."

"Betcha can't," she said.

"You really want—"

"I really want you, Jeremy. Come to me now."

She opened her arms and her legs, inviting him

into her body. He lowered himself over her and rubbed against her. Shifted until he'd caressed every part of her.

She reached between his legs and cupped him in her hands, and he shuddered. "Not now. Or I won't last."

She smiled up at him. "Really?"

He wanted to hug her close at the look of wonder on her face. "Hell, yes."

He needed to be inside her *now*. He lifted her thighs, wrapping her legs around his waist. Her hands fluttered between them and their eyes met.

He held her hips steady and entered her slowly until he was fully seated. Her eyes widened with each inch he gave her. She clutched at his hips as he started to move.

He leaned down and caught one of her nipples in his teeth, scraping very gently. She started to tighten around him. Her hips moving faster, demanding more, but he kept the pace slow, steady, wanting to feel her climax again before he did.

He suckled her nipple and rotated his hips to catch her pleasure point with each thrust. Her hands clenched in his hair and she threw her head back as her climax ripped through her.

He leaned back on his haunches and tipped her hips up to give him deeper access. Her body was still clenching around his when he felt that tightening at the base of his spine seconds before his body erupted into hers. He pounded into her two, three more times then collapsed against her, careful to keep his weight from crushing her. He rolled to his side, taking her with him.

He kept his head at her breast and smoothed his hands down her back, realizing he'd just made a colossal mistake.

Having sex with Bella hadn't lessened his obsession with her. It had deepened it.

Jeremy got out of the bed and padded into the bathroom. Bella stared up at the ceiling, her entire body tingling from his lovemaking. She'd never expected it to be like this. *This* was beyond anything she'd experienced. She was pulsing.

He came back into the room and climbed back in the bed, then propped the pillows up at the head and drew her into his arms, not saying anything.

She had no idea what to do now.

"What are you thinking?" He finally broke the silence.

"That you are incredible."

"Incredible, eh? I like the sound of that."

"Great, just what you need. Another reason to be arrogant."

He tipped her head back and lowered his mouth to hers. His kisses overwhelmed her. They should both be sated and not interested in making love again. Yet as his tongue played in her mouth, she felt the rekindling of her own desire. She wanted him again. She tried to angle her head to reciprocate, but he held her still.

This was his embrace and she felt the fierce need in him to dominate her. To remind her that she was his. She'd found the proof she was searching for that Jeremy was different from every other man she'd ever met.

His biceps flexed as he shifted her in his arms, rolling her under him and then running his hands over her body.

His mouth moved down the column of her neck, nibbling and biting softly. He lingered at the base of her neck, where her pulse beat frantically. Then he sucked on her skin. Everything in her body clenched. Not enough to push her over the edge, just enough to make her frantic for more of him.

She scored his shoulders with her fingernails before skimming them down his chest, caressing his flat male nipples as he held himself above her on his strong arms. She liked the way she was surrounded by him, feeling very feminine as she lay there under him. His skin was hot to the touch and she wrapped her arms around his body, pulling him closer.

He pulled back, staring down at her. Then he traced one finger over the full globes of her breasts. She shifted her shoulders, inviting his caress. He took one of her nipples between his thumb and forefinger, pinching lightly.

She shook with need. Couldn't wait for him.

She reached between their bodies, but he shifted his hips out of her reach. His mouth fastened on her left nipple, suckling her strongly. She undulated against him, her hips lifting toward him. He drew his other hand down her body, his fingers tangling in the hair at her center.

He caressed her between her legs until she was frantically holding his head to her breasts, trying to find a release that remained just out of reach. She skimmed her hands down his body.

His breath hissed out as she reached between his legs to cup him and caress his length.

"There's a condom in the nightstand."

"Hmm…mmm," she said, too busy exploring him to really pay attention to what he said.

"Bella, baby, you're killing me."

She liked the sound of that. The way his breath caught whenever she gently scored him with her nails. He shifted over her, opening the nightstand drawer and pulling out a condom.

"Put it on me."

"With pleasure."

She opened the package before she remembered she hadn't done this before. But it wasn't that hard to figure out. He groaned as she covered him, and she thought maybe she'd done it right.

She started to reach lower again but he caught her hand and stretched it over her head. He lifted her leg up around his hip, shifted his body. She felt him hot, hard and ready at her entrance. But he made no move to take her. She looked up at him.

"You're mine."

She couldn't respond to that. "I…"

"Watch me take you, Bella, and know that this means that you belong to me."

He thrust inside her then. Lifted her up, holding her with his big hands as he repeatedly drove into her. He went deeper than he had earlier. She felt too full, stretched and surrounded by him.

He bit her neck carefully and sucked against her skin and everything tightened inside her until she felt another climax spread through her body. Her skin was pulsing, her body tightening around him. A moment later he came, crying her name and holding her tightly to his chest.

She rested her head against his shoulder and held him. Wrapped completely around his body, she realized the truth of what he'd said. She was his.

Eight

The phone rang just after lunch and Bella hesitated to answer it. Shelley had been in her office twice trying to pump her for more information on her date. And Bella didn't want to share those details with anyone. She wanted to hold them close.

Plus, despite their synchronicity in bed, there was still tension between her and Jeremy.

She struggled to keep that romantic dinner under the Chihuly glass in her mental scrapbook as one of the best meals of her entire life. There were so few in that category. And most of them had happened a long time ago, when both of her parents were still alive.

The phone stopped ringing and then the intercom buzzed.

"Yes, Shelley."

"Dare's on the line. Why didn't you pick up?"

"I'm working on a proposal," she said, which was partially true. She'd spoken to Jeremy's personal chef, Andy Conti, earlier and she was in the process of planning the details of his yacht party as a surprise to him. He'd given her so many gifts and she thought this would be a nice way to give back to him.

Andy said it was a casual event. But from their discussion, she knew it wasn't her idea of a casual event, where she offered to grill chicken and her friends brought over side dishes and bottles of wine.

She wanted every detail of Jeremy's party to be perfect. She knew Lucinda would be there. Bella figured this was her chance to show how well she fit in Jeremy's world.

"Hey, sis." She heard old-school Beastie Boys playing in the background. "No Sleep Till Brooklyn." She loved that song and had introduced her brother to the group when he'd come home with a Tupac CD.

"What's up? And can you turn the radio down?"

The volume immediately was lowered. "I'm coming home this weekend with a few friends and I'm planning to crash at your place. Is that okay?"

"Dare, it's your place, too." She liked that he

asked, but he didn't need to. She still missed him around the house. Even though he'd only lived with her off and on since she'd moved to her current place, she was still used to thinking of it as their home.

"Not anymore. I'm subleasing a place in Manhattan."

"Can you afford it?" she asked, but she knew he could. He had matured so much in the last few years. She didn't like the thought of him living so far away. She'd always had Dare close by. And New York wasn't close.

She was alone. Really alone, she thought.

"Yes, sis, I can. I'm going to be making big bucks at my new job."

"Don't spend it before you've earned it," she warned him. She'd taken several money management classes after her mom had declared bankruptcy. She hated that feeling of having nothing. Of watching strangers come in and take everything they'd owned and sell it to pay their debts.

"I'm not. We both learned that lesson the hard way, didn't we?"

She took a deep breath and smiled to herself. She still thought of him as a rebellious boy even though he'd straightened up his act. "Yes, we did."

"I want you to plan a trip to the city to visit me this fall after I've settled in."

"I will."

Dare really had turned out okay. There had been

a time—well, three and a half years ago—when he was running wild and getting arrested, that she'd thought she was going to end up visiting him in jail.

"I've got something on Saturday. Do you still have your key?"

"Yes. What are you doing?"

For some reason she didn't want to mention Jeremy's name. "A yacht party."

"One of your wealthy clients again?"

"Um…not exactly."

"A date? Bella, who are you dating?" He was teasing her and she wanted to laugh with him but wasn't sure how he'd react.

"Jeremy."

"Mr. Harper?"

"Do we know any other Jeremy?" she asked a little sarcastically, because she was nervous.

"No. Are you sure you know what you're doing?"

No, she had absolutely no idea what she was doing. But at this point she wasn't going to back out. And after last night, she'd confirmed that she wanted a lot longer with Jeremy than a mere six months.

"Sis?"

"What?"

"Be careful."

"I've been taking care of us for a long time."

"Yes, you have, and now that I'm older it's time I stepped up and watched out for you."

"Jeremy's not a bad guy."

"I'm not saying that. But he is a smooth operator and you're not his normal type of woman."

"What's that supposed to mean?" she asked, not exactly sure where her brother was going with this.

"Just that you've been busy taking care of me and haven't done a lot of dating. He's a pretty experienced man, remember that."

"I will."

"I like him. He's done a lot of good things for us, but that doesn't mean he's family."

"I know that, Dare. I don't think he understands how to let anyone close."

"And you don't know how to keep anyone at arm's length once you get to know them."

"What time will you be here on Saturday?" she asked, forcibly changing the subject.

"Sometime after lunch. Don't forget what I said."

"I won't."

She couldn't believe Dare was giving her advice. But it warmed her heart in ways she'd never be able to articulate. For so long they'd struggled and now…now she felt that they were both going to make it. And she knew they both had one man to thank…Jeremy Harper.

Jeremy wasn't sure what to expect when he arrived at Bella's house. She'd sent him a text message earlier saying that she had a weekly dinner she couldn't cancel. Since they'd spent the last two nights making love, he figured they were due for more socializing.

And it would do him good to be around other people. His focus on her was becoming too narrow. He kept feeling like he was never going to get enough of her, which wasn't helping his obsession at all. No matter how often he made love to her, he still wanted her. No matter how many hours he held her in his arms, he still felt like six months wasn't going to be long enough.

She'd told him to bring a bottle of wine and to dress casually. He heard the sound of voices and music coming from the backyard when he arrived. He recognized Kenny Chesney's song, "No Shoes, No Shirt, No Problems."

He walked around back carrying the wine he'd picked up in France when he'd been there on business two weeks ago. As soon as he came around the corner he saw a group of ten or so people sitting around the pool.

He hesitated, remembering Kell and Lucinda's reactions toward Bella. His friends hadn't been exactly welcoming. How would her friends react to him? Did he want to know her outside of their agreement? He was a step away from turning around when she stepped out of the house onto the patio and saw him.

She smiled and it lit up her entire face. He wasn't

leaving, no matter how much he might want to. This was definitely crossing the line beyond what he'd outlined in their contract. But when she waved at him, he simply walked toward her.

Everyone stopped talking and he felt like he was on display, but that was nothing new. He ignored it as best he could.

"I'm so glad you made it," Bella said, wrapping one arm around his waist and leaning up to give him a kiss on his cheek. He turned his head and captured her lips.

Then stepped away. "Where do you want the wine?"

"Over there. Charlie is manning the bar. Let me put this down and I'll introduce you to everyone."

He handed the bottle of wine to Charlie, who shook his hand. She introduced him to the rest of her friends and he found them to be an inviting and eclectic group, ranging from business professionals such as an accountant and a stockbroker to a romance novelist and her animator husband to a couple who ran a tourist sailing operation.

Jeremy was comfortable with the group and found himself falling easily into the role of host by the time the evening ended and everyone left. But despite the fact that he was enjoying himself, he didn't like the fact that he and Bella were clearly a couple here.

Bella smiled and held his arm as the last couple walked to their car. "That was fun. Next week we're supposed to go to Charlie's house. Will you be available?"

"Ah, I don't know. I'll have to check my schedule," he said. He didn't want to isolate her from her life and her friends, but he was struggling to keep her in the box labeled *mistress,* and hanging out with her friends wasn't going to help.

"Okay. Just let me know if you can make it."

"It seems like an odd group."

"Kind of. We've been meeting for about two years now. It started out being just a few of us, hanging out at Chili's, but then we decided we could hear each other better at home."

"You're not much for going out, are you?" he asked, realizing that she always suggested something in.

"No."

"Why not?"

She shrugged and turned aside to gather up some empty wineglasses.

"Tell me, Bella."

"For a long time people used to stare at us. Dad's death was front-page news."

He couldn't imagine what that had been like. "I read some articles about him."

"He wasn't like they said in those articles. He really loved our family and he was such a dreamer. He just had no head for business. Eventually he lost all he'd inherited."

"What do you remember most about him?"

"He hated to be away from us. When he'd come home, the first thing he'd do was give Mom and me a big hug and then we'd all sit around the table and talk."

"Was he gone a lot?"

"Yes…more and more that last year."

"I'm sorry."

"It's been a long time."

"But it doesn't go away, does it?"

"No, it doesn't. And people don't stare anymore. I just got used to staying home."

He looked around her house. It was smaller than his, and not decorated with designer furniture, but it was warm and cozy. He liked the looks of the overstuffed sofa and could easily imagine sitting there with her.

"I think the Heat are playing tonight. You can probably catch the end of the game if you want to."

"Do you want to watch it?"

"After I'm done cleaning up. Dare and I try to watch all the games. He e-mails with his highlights and asks for mine."

"I'll help you," he said.

"You don't have to help. You're my guest."

He didn't say anything to that, just started gathering plates to clear the table. "Have you been to a Heat game?"

"Yes, a few. But my business is unpredictable, so I don't have season tickets."

"I have tickets with Kell and Daniel. The next home game, we'll go."

"I'd like that."

He gathered up the plates from the table on the patio and loaded them into the dishwasher. She didn't say anything as they worked and soon they had the place clean. They put on the game and finished the bottle of wine he'd brought. He wrapped one arm around her and held her close to him.

She fell asleep before the game ended and he shifted her into his arms and carried her down the hall to her bedroom. He didn't want to think about tonight or the feelings she evoked in him. So instead he took off her clothes, waking her up. He took off his own and joined her on the bed, making love to her.

She fell asleep in his arms and he stared at the wall for most of the night, wondering how his carefully crafted plan had gone so wrong.

The next few weeks flew by and Bella felt that each step she took toward making Jeremy view her as more than a temporary mistress was countered by an obstacle either from her past or his friends. She carefully avoided Lucinda at any events where she and Daniel were in attendance. And Jeremy's cousin Kell spent a lot of time talking to her about prenups and the advantages on both sides.

Which made her sad, because it was clear that he thought she was only after Jeremy for his money. If he knew how well Jeremy had protected himself against that, she suspected Kell would back off. And that made her more emotional, because she sensed that Jeremy cared enough about her to keep quiet about the mistress contract.

Yet he didn't care enough to say that they didn't need a contract between them any longer. Honestly, that was what she really wanted. She reminded herself of the contract to keep a certain distance between them. To protect herself from allowing her emotions to get the better of it. But it wasn't working.

She glanced around the elegant ballroom, no longer feeling out of place. Lucinda had cornered her once and Jeremy had rescued her. It was one of the most heroic things he'd done for her. But now she was alone again, in a beautiful Oscar de la Renta gown that Jeremy had given her.

"Somehow I didn't expect to find you hiding out on the terrace."

Kell walked over to her. He looked very elegant and sophisticated in his tuxedo. Handsome, but not as attractive to her as Jeremy was.

"Jeremy asked me to wait here." She was situated behind large potted trees that had been filled with twinkling lights. From her vantage point she had a view of the entire room, but no one else could really see her.

"Now it all makes sense," Kell said. "This is one of our favorite spots."

"Favorite spots for what?" she asked.

"Hiding out," he said with a wry grin. Kell could be charming when he tried.

She opened her small handbag and took out an article on prenups she'd clipped from the *Wall Street Journal* a few days ago. "I saw this and thought of you."

He took the article, glanced down at it. A brief smile touched his lips. "You're not what I expected."

She still hoped that her relationship would outlast the three months remaining on the mistress contract. And if it was going to have a chance to survive, she knew she needed to make more of an effort with Jeremy's friends. He didn't do a lot with them but she knew they were important to him—especially Kell.

"Well, I think all of us gold diggers are a little bit different."

He arched one eyebrow at her. "Jeremy doesn't see you that way."

"Then why do you?" she asked.

"Let's just say I've been there."

She finally saw more than a good-looking, successful man in Kell and it was more than a little disheartening to realize she'd been so shallow. "I'm sorry. I care about Jeremy."

"I've noticed that."

"Why did you think I was a gold digger?" she asked.

He shrugged.

She knew that she should stop this line of questioning, but she had to know. What had he heard about her? Please don't let it about the mistress contract, she thought. She'd absolutely die of embarrassment if all of his friends knew that they weren't in a real relationship.

"Tell me. It can't be anything I haven't heard before."

"It wasn't anything about you," he said. "Jeremy would kick my butt if he heard me talking to you about this."

"Well, he's not here," she said carefully. She was almost a hundred-percent positive that whatever Kell had heard he'd mentioned to Jeremy. So he already knew whatever damaging gossip Kell had told him about her. And it had to be gossip, because she hadn't done anything for money that she regretted.

"You'd keep secrets from him?" he asked. Immediately he lost his charm and she saw the barracuda look in his eyes. She'd heard he was a corporate attorney who never lost a case and she could see why. There was an utter ruthlessness in his gaze.

She sighed. "No, I wouldn't."

"Of course she wouldn't, Kell. What are you two talking about?"

She accepted the Bellini from Jeremy and

took a sip of the smooth peach-and-champagne drink. Jeremy wrapped an arm around her waist and pulled her firmly to his side.

"Um…"

"Gold diggers."

"Not that again," Jeremy said under his breath.

"I wanted to know what he'd heard about me to make him believe I'd be after your money."

"It was old news about your family," Jeremy said.

From Lucinda. She was the only one who would have known all the sordid details. The papers had reported that a business deal had gone wrong and her father, distraught from it, had killed himself. But the truth was a little darker. Her father had somehow gotten involved with the mob in a shady deal that she didn't know all the details of. She could only imagine how desperate he must have been. The day after her father's suicide, the DEA had arrived at the door to seize all of their property in connection with her father's business dealings.

Even the papers hadn't gotten all the details. But her dear friend Lucinda had, because Bella had told her.

Tears burned in the back of her eyes. She didn't think she could still feel betrayed from that long-ago friendship. But of course she could. At one time, Lucinda had been like a sister to her.

"Thanks for telling me. Does anyone else know?"

"Just Daniel, and he won't repeat it," Kell said. "Neither would I. It's not anything personal—"

"I know," she said, putting her hand on his arm to stop him. "You were just looking out for Jeremy."

"I can look out for myself," Jeremy said wryly.

Kell didn't say anything, just kept watching her with that stare of his. Finally she sighed and said, "I can't blame you there."

Kell nodded at her and then left. Jeremy drew her back against his solid frame, not saying another word. She let the strength in his body surround her and soothe the wounds left over from Lucinda.

Nine

Jeremy watched Kell walk away. He'd known that Kell didn't trust Bella, but he had no idea that the two of them had spent so much time chatting alone. He knew that Bella could handle herself, but he should have paid closer attention to Kell.

"Sorry if he was being a pain."

She took another sip of her drink and glanced sideways at him. Her hair slid along the sleeve of his tuxedo jacket and he wished they were home alone so he could feel her hair on his skin. She had the softest hair.

"He wasn't. It's sweet the way he tries to take care of you."

"*Sweet?* I don't think anyone would describe Kell that way."

They watched as Kell stopped to speak with his sister, Lorraine, and her group. Her women friends all moved subtly, trying to attract his attention. One woman tossed her hair, another touched his arm.

"He does have that barracuda smile—you know, all teeth—that makes you feel like you're about to be eaten, but underneath that...he watches out for you. Why is that?" she asked.

His relationship with Kell was deep and complex. He doubted that either of them would know how to explain it. But they'd been alone a lot with the same lazy nanny and they'd spent a lot of their time escaping her. "He's six months older than I am. And his mom used to make him promise to watch me."

Almost absently he remembered the long days of summer when their mothers would spend afternoons on the beach drinking fruity concoctions and gossiping while he and Kell ran free like wild boys.

"I remember you mentioning that his side of the family was goofy."

He grimaced at his old joke. He shouldn't have said that. Most people were unaware that Kell's mother was a recluse, prone to depression. For as much as he had happy memories of his childhood, it was also tinged with memories of Aunt Mary's "sadness," as his mother called it. They'd often rushed to her house so that his mom could cheer her up.

He suspected his mother used Aunt Mary's illness to ignore the fact that Jeremy's dad spent more time with his mistress than with them.

It didn't always work. His childhood memories were clouded with the secrets of his aunt Mary's depression and Kell coming to live with them for months at a time. He wouldn't share that with Bella. Some secrets weren't his to tell.

Just as Lucinda should have kept quiet about Bella's family. He'd said as much to Daniel.

"That's because my branch of the family isn't crazy," he said.

She looked steadily at him. "I think there's more to it than what you just said."

Jeremy shrugged, not really comfortable talking about Kell or his relationship with him. But there were some things he wanted to share with Bella. She quietly accepted everything about him. Even his flaws.

Whenever he was with her, he felt…complete. Which made no sense to him. He'd been happy with his life before they'd become lovers. Now he didn't like to think about what going back to life without Bella would be like.

"Tell me," she said. She wrapped one arm around his waist and glanced up at him expectantly.

"He saved my life one time."

"Literally?"

"Yes." A sailing accident that had surprised Jeremy. He'd always been at home on the water. But he'd been hit by the boom as they'd changed direction and been knocked overboard. One minute he'd been on the yacht, and the next thing he remembered was Kell's hand on his wrist, pulling him to the surface.

She cupped his jaw, bringing him back to the present. He glanced down into her honey-brown eyes. There was such a well of caring there that he felt like he'd taken a punch to the gut.

"I'm so glad he saved you," she said, raising up on tiptoe and kissing him. It was a soft and sweet kiss. The kind that made him glad to be alive and holding this woman in his arms.

"Me, too," he said. Never more so than this moment.

From the first time he'd met Bella, he'd sensed she was different from other women. At first he'd thought it was because she was no longer part of the moneyed set he ran in. But the more time he spent with her, the more he realized that she had an innate innocence that drew him to her.

He knew she wasn't innocent, that her life had been carved out of emotionally tough events. But she'd retained a certain sweetness that she showered on those around her. And he thanked God that he'd been fortunate enough to bind her to him when he had.

They only had three months left on their contract. His gut tightened at the thought of her leaving him. He needed to start planning for the next phase of their relationship, but he had no idea what that would entail.

"You ready to get out of here?"

"You did promise me a dance."

And he realized, as he deposited their drinks on a tray and led her to the dance floor, that he never wanted to break a promise he made to her.

She and Jeremy stayed for another half hour before they left the party. Twice Lucinda had made eye contact with her and indicated she wanted to talk. But Bella's evening had been perfect and she hadn't wanted to ruin it, so she'd ignored her onetime friend.

Jeremy put the top down on the convertible and drove them to the beach. It was a Saturday night and luckily she didn't have to work tomorrow. He held her hand loosely on his thigh.

Everything felt just about perfect, and that worried her. Because whenever she got too comfortable, something bad happened. And she was depending a lot on Jeremy—more than she wanted.

When she'd signed the contract with Jeremy she hadn't been too sure what she expected. Maybe a chance to reclaim something that had been stolen from her as a young woman. But she'd found so much more.

Did he feel the same? Sometimes she sensed he did, though it was true that he kept part of himself from her. He didn't speak of emotions or longevity—but neither did she.

Part of her was afraid to rock the boat. She was used to her life being constantly in flux, never taking anything for granted, but there was something very solid and reassuring about Jeremy and his presence in her life. And she wanted to believe that he was going to be a permanent addition to it.

She'd never been in love before, but she was falling for Jeremy.

"Deep thoughts?" he asked.

She shook her head, frantically trying to think of something to say that wouldn't leave her vulnerable to him. "Just enjoying the night and the wind in my hair."

He lifted her hand to his mouth, brushing a kiss along her knuckles. She liked that he was accepting of the limits she placed, that he didn't push her past them. Of course, it was different when they were in bed. There he would stand no barriers between them.

He'd pushed her further than she'd ever expected to go with any man. He made her give him everything she had, and never let her hide behind her own inhibitions.

"Then you're going to love what I have planned for us."

"What is it?" she asked. This was yet another instance that gave her hope. He was being very romantic and not at all businesslike about their relationship. After he'd offered her the town house, she expected him to focus on just the sexual side of things. Instead, he was always romancing her, planning evenings that fulfilled secret dreams she'd scarcely realized she had.

"A surprise," he said, slowing the car as they turned into the yacht club.

"I don't like surprises." But she did like going out on his yacht. She'd realized fairly early in her relationship with Jeremy that he was most at peace at sea. He liked to entertain on his boat, sleep on his boat, hold her on his boat. He never said much about it, but she could see a difference in him as soon as they motored out to sea.

"Or gifts," he said.

"I like your gifts. It's just that they're so extravagant." He'd overwhelmed her with the gifts he'd given her during the last three months. Some of the gifts were jewelry, which she half expected, but others were sentimental. Such as her mother's classic '69 Mustang, which had been sold to a collector to pay off some of their debts years ago. The collector had put it in storage and left it intact; their mom had been the last one to drive it.

She had so many memories of that car. Sometimes she just sat in the backseat and felt a little closer to her mom. Even Dare had been rendered speechless by the car.

He rubbed the diamond tennis bracelet that he'd given her earlier this evening. "I like you in diamonds."

"Is that why you insisted I wear the choker tonight?" she asked, lifting her free hand to touch the band of diamonds around her neck.

"Yes," he said, parking the car in his assigned spot. "Now, tell me what you were really thinking about."

She sighed. They were getting too close to each other. He saw parts of her that she normally hid away.

"You know me too well."

"Not yet. But soon I'll have all your secrets figured out."

"I'm not sure I like the sound of that."

"Why not? Don't you trust me?"

She did trust him on one level. She knew that, unlike Lucinda, Jeremy would never reveal anything personal about her to the world. But that didn't mean that he was planning to stick around for the long haul. And if he still left after three months, she was going to have to deal with the fact that her trust in him had been misplaced.

"Ah, that's a telling silence," he said. It was impossible to tell what he was thinking from his tone. He was a master at hiding his emotions. She wished she had that same ability. Everything she felt seemed to be broadcast like a twenty-four-hour news channel.

"It's not so much that I don't trust you."

"Then what is it?"

She took a deep breath. How could she say that every day they spent together made her wish time could stand still? "I'm afraid of what will happen when you're gone."

"Your secrets will always be safe with me."

"Yes, but I won't always be with you and I'm not sure I'm ready to think about that."

He pulled his hand free and got out of the car without another word. She watched him walk away from her. His stride was angry and she couldn't blame him, but they both had to acknowledge that there was a clock ticking as far as their relationship was concerned.

And so far he hadn't made any overt indication that he was interested in keeping her around any longer, despite their growing closeness. She wasn't going to pretend that her life was one thing when she knew it was something else.

Jeremy heard her footsteps behind him and turned to make sure her heels didn't get caught in the tiny cracks between the boards on the dock. He shouldn't have left her alone in the car. The flash of anger had surprised him.

Even as a child he'd always been even-keeled.

But with Bella so many reactions were unexpected. Even their lovemaking, though satisfying, always made him yearn for her again.

"Jeremy…"

There was a sadness in her voice that he couldn't stand hearing. He knew that she'd only given him the truth he'd asked her for. He had the same fears. Sharing so much of himself with her was bound to leave them both hurting when the relationship ended.

"No more talking tonight."

"I didn't mean to ruin the evening."

He was being an ass and he knew it. "You didn't. I'm just not ready to talk about our relationship being over."

"Me neither," she said softly.

He walked back to her. "Wait here."

He went back to his car and grabbed their overnight bags from the trunk, then locked it. Bella stood on the dock looking out to sea. She was good at keeping her true feelings and thoughts to herself. Too good.

The only time he felt her guard drop was when he made love to her.

He didn't say anything, just walked with her to his slip and lifted her aboard his boat. He untied the lines that held the boat in place and then climbed aboard. She took their bags to the stateroom as he prepared to leave the marina.

"Do you want a drink?" she called from below deck.

"No," he said. What he wanted he doubted he could ever have. He wanted everything she had to give. He wanted it from the safety of the relationship they had.

He knew that wasn't fair. But he'd designed this relationship so he'd have all the advantages. He was only now realizing he'd forgotten a few things.

"Are you going to stay mad at me all night?" she asked from right behind him. Her hair blew around her face and shoulders in the light breeze. The skirt of her dress swirled around her legs.

"I don't know," he said honestly, because watching her standing there brought home to him how far out of reach she really was. He could hold her and make love to her, but it was temporary.

"I'd rather go home than spend the night with you acting like this."

Screw that. He wasn't going to waste one night of the three months they had left together. He wanted her by his side for all of them. "I don't want you to go home."

She smiled at him, that fey little grin that he never could read, and took a few steps closer to him. "I don't want you to be sulky."

"I sound like an eight-year-old when you put it that way."

"Well…" She stopped in front of him, placing her hands around his neck. She rested her body against his and spoke softly against his skin. He felt each word the instant she said it. "You don't resemble an eight-year-old."

He wrapped his arms around her, lowering his head to the top of hers and just breathing her in. He rested his hands at the small of her back, nestling them together until not an inch of space separated them.

"I'm acting like one?" he asked, brushing his lips along the column of her neck. He traced the line of the choker with his tongue. God, she was beautiful. If she ever had an inkling of how he felt toward her…fear gripped him. He didn't want to let her go. Not tonight. Not in three months. Not ever.

"I guess I was being pretty childish, too, keeping secrets," she said, tipping her head back so that their eyes met.

But she hadn't been. He knew how hard it was for her to let anyone close to her, despite the fact that she had a large circle of friends. There were very few people that she actually let know the real woman.

And he wanted to be one of those few.

She trailed her fingers over his jaw, then down his chest. She laid her head there, right over his heart. He tightened his arms around her. Held her as close as he could without saying a word.

He didn't want to talk anymore. Why had he started a conversation that went where he didn't want it to go?

"In the car, I was thinking about this."

"Making love?" he asked, leaning down to kiss her. Sex was on his mind most of the time when they were together. Hell, even when they were apart he was thinking about how it felt to have her in his arms. The soft sounds she made when he thrust into her body and how she wrapped herself around him when they finished.

He lifted his head, brushing his lips along the curve of her cheek down to her neck. He suckled at the smooth, soft skin, wanting to leave his mark there. Wanting in some way to brand her as his so that everyone she met knew she was taken.

Taken by him. His, he thought. Really his, and not just for a few months.

She smiled up at him. "In a way."

She took a step away from him, wrapping her arms around her waist and staring out at sea. He hated how she could isolate herself from him in one movement. He stepped up behind her, pulling her back against him.

"What way?"

"I was thinking about how quickly the last three months have gone by, and wishing that the next three months never had to end."

Jeremy smiled at her, but words stuck in his throat. Could he risk being that honest and open about wanting her?

Ten

Jeremy woke the next morning, scrubbing a hand over his face and staring at the woman lying curled so close to him. Her confession last night had set a fire in him he hadn't been able to put out. Something had started winding its way unexpectedly into his life.

She'd organized a couple of parties for him, acting as his hostess. He knew she did some business at the parties, drumming up new clientele, but mainly she acted the way his mother always had at his father's business functions. And that unnerved him.

He wasn't ready for their relationship to end, yet at the same time those three months couldn't come fast enough. He felt like this relationship was unraveling, and he had no idea how to get it back on the track he'd planned.

He pushed himself out of bed—because he wanted to linger.

"Jeremy?"

"Right here," he said, sinking back down next to her. If he wasn't careful they'd spend the rest of the weekend together on the boat, in bed.

"Is it morning already?" she asked, leaning over to kiss his chest. He shifted so that he lay next to her, his morning hard-on pressing against her hip. He shouldn't want her again so soon. He'd had her three times last night.

"Yes." He took her mouth with his, letting his hands wander over her body.

Her stomach growled and he laughed. "Hungry?"

She buried her red face against his chest. "Yes. I didn't eat at the party last night."

"Maybe that's because you kept trying to avoid Lucinda." He pulled the sheet back from the bed and reached for one of the silk bindings he'd used to tie her to the bed the night before, trailing it over her torso and breasts.

She shivered with awareness and her nipples tightened. He arranged the silk binding over her breasts. "I wish you hadn't noticed that."

He leaned down to lick each nipple. Then he blew gently on the tips. She raked her nails down his back.

"Are you listening to me?" she asked.

"To your body," he said.

He knelt between her thighs and looked down at her. "Open yourself for me," he said.

Her legs moved but he took her hands in his, brought them to her mound.

"Lift your hips, honey."

He leaned down, blowing lightly on her. She lifted her hips toward his mouth.

He drew her flesh into his mouth, sucking carefully on her. He pushed his finger into her body and lifted his head to look up at her.

Her eyes were closed, her head tipped back. Her shoulders arched, throwing her breasts forward with their hard tips, begging for more attention. Her entire body was a creamy delight.

He lowered his head again, hungry for more of her, using his teeth, tongue and fingers to bring her to the brink of climax, but held her there, wanting to draw out the moment of completion until she was begging him for it.

"Jeremy, please."

He slid deep into her. She arched her back, reaching up to entwine her arms around his shoulders. He thrust harder and felt every nerve in his body tensing. Reaching between their bodies, he touched her between her legs until he felt her body tighten around him.

He came in a rush, continuing to thrust into her

until his body was drained. He then collapsed on top of her, laying his head between her breasts.

He turned his face away from her, afraid to admit that something had changed between them overnight, but knowing that he wasn't going to let her go. He was going to find a way to keep her at his side.

The next few months flew by. Jeremy became a part of her life in a way she hadn't predicted. After their intense night together, neither of them had mentioned the contract or the fact that they didn't want to end their relationship after six months.

But that didn't bother her. Jeremy was everything she'd always wanted in a man and more. She didn't know when her dreams for the future had been reborn. But she found herself thinking of long-term plans instead of dwelling on what had been taken from her.

This afternoon was a perfect example. It was Jeremy's birthday and she'd planned a surprise party for him. Kell, despite his initial misgivings about her, had warmed considerably in the last few weeks and had helped her with the guest list. The party was going to be at her home.

She'd never have been able to do this with his circle of friends even a month ago. But it had felt right for this event. Jeremy seemed to like her house, and catering a party for him at his place felt too presumptuous. She really wanted this to be a special day.

He was turning thirty-five, a milestone that he'd mentioned to her one time and then let drop. His parents were flying home early from Europe to come to the party. They had been surprised when she'd called. Apparently Jeremy hadn't mentioned her to them.

She was a little nervous about that. She'd never met his parents, and she knew she and Jeremy weren't really dating.

"This place looks great."

She glanced at Dare. She was always a little startled to see him looking like a man. For so long he'd been that half-wild boy with eyes that broke her heart. Now she saw wisdom and maturity in him. "Yes, it does. Did you get those extra bags of ice?"

"Yes. And I made another run to the liquor store, so the bar is overstocked. Quit worrying, sis. You've thrown thousands of parties." He put his arm around her shoulder and they stood together in the living room of her home.

"But this one is different," she said. She'd never really hid anything from Dare. Not this Dare anyway. The teenage rebel he'd been hadn't been interested in anyone except himself.

Dare looked at her like she was crazy. "You really like Mr. Harper?"

"Yes, I do."

He hugged her close and then went over to the mantel to adjust a framed picture of the two of them from last summer. "I'm glad, Bella. I'm really glad."

"Why?" she asked. It wasn't like Dare to adjust anything.

"It makes it easier to take that job in New York."

She had an inkling of where Dare was going with this conversation. "Why would it?"

"Because you won't be alone."

She shook her head at him. "I'm never alone. I have a very busy life."

"Yes, you do. But you didn't have anyone to take care of while I was gone, and now you do."

His words gave her pause. Was that the main attraction she felt toward Jeremy? The fact that he let her take care of him, and she'd been searching for a long time for someone who would? "He's good to me, too."

"Glad to hear it."

The doorbell rang and soon the party guests started arriving. Daniel and Lucinda arrived in the midst of her friends from her weekly dinner. She didn't have to greet them individually, but Bella was tired of avoiding her childhood friend. Tired of running from the lies and the hateful things they'd both said.

Lucinda was standing in a mixed group of some

of her friends and Jeremy's business partners. Bella started over toward the crowd. Lucinda glanced up at her and excused herself from the others to meet her halfway.

"Bella, thank you for inviting me."

"You're welcome. I...well, I'm sure you noticed I've been avoiding you."

Lucinda laughed, and it was a kind sound. It reminded Bella of their childhood and how much fun they'd once had together.

"Yes, I have. I think I had something to do with that. I'm sorry for telling Kell and Daniel the details about your dad."

"I wish you hadn't," she said. But Bella was surprised that she didn't feel that knot in the bottom of her stomach that she always had when she thought of someone finding out about her past.

"Well, I did. It was in bad taste and I have no excuse except that I was so shocked to see you. Last time I saw you, you and your mother were cleaning my house."

There was something in Lucinda's voice that Bella had never noticed before. It sounded almost like anger. "Why does that bother you?"

She shrugged. "I hate what your dad did. He stole my best friend from me. And I'm still mad at myself for not being a better friend to you."

"I don't think I could have handled it then. I felt so destroyed and unsure of myself."

"I'm sorry. I'm really sorry for how I acted back then and for bringing it up again."

Bella forgave her friend, knowing that a portion of the blame sat on her own shoulders. "Don't worry about mentioning it to Kell. He researched me on the Internet anyway."

Lucinda started laughing and Bella noticed Daniel glancing over at them. "He did the same thing when Daniel and I started dating."

"I guess we can't fault him for caring about the men we like."

Lucinda took her hand and drew her into a corner away from everyone else. "I'm glad you're with Jeremy, but…"

"What?" she asked, almost afraid to hear what Lucinda might say.

"Be careful with your heart, Bella. Jeremy always moves on."

"I know that. But I think maybe I'm changing his way of thinking."

"I hope so. I'm looking forward to having my old friend back in my life. Even if things don't work out with Jeremy," Lucinda said.

Bella was, too. She'd renewed many acquaintances from her childhood these past few months and it had felt right to be back in that circle. Some of the people she had nothing in common with, but others were turning into good friends. It had made her realize how much she'd missed the social part of her old life.

The door opened before she could respond and Jeremy walked in. She saw the surprise on his face as everyone broke out into a chorus of the birthday song. He didn't greet his parents or his friends first but made a beeline to her side, pulling her into his arms and kissing her.

Everyone broke into applause and Bella felt like she'd found something that she'd spent a lifetime searching for. And she was certain that Jeremy realized it, too.

The party lasted until after midnight. Kell's and Jeremy's mothers were the last to leave. His dad had left early for a meeting, which Jeremy knew meant he was going to see his mistress. His mom really liked Bella and had taken him aside three separate times to tell him so. Finally the last guest left and he and Bella were alone.

"Thank you," he said when they'd finished cleaning up and were sharing a glass of wine on her patio. He pulled her down on the glider next to him, keeping her tucked close to his side.

"Were you surprised?"

"Yes," he said.

"Good. I know how much you like surprises."

"I like surprising you," he said quietly.

"I think I know why. It was so much fun planning this and waiting to see how you would react to it."

He didn't say anything else, realizing he didn't

want to talk. He tipped her head back against his shoulder and leaned down to kiss her. She tasted of the sweet wine they were drinking and of something unique to her. He loved that taste. Couldn't ever get enough of it. He shifted around until he could place the wineglass on the floor and then maneuvered her sideways on his lap so he could caress her while they were kissing.

He'd never let anyone be a part of his life the way he had with Bella. Tonight had brought that home in many ways. His mother liked her. Even Kell, who was leery of all women and treated most of them with disdain, was starting to soften toward her, though he still seemed wary of Jeremy getting suckered in.

He lifted his head, rubbing his thumb over her lower lip. It was moist and swollen from his kisses. "What were you and Lucinda talking about?"

She shrugged, laying her head on his shoulder. Her fingers traced a random pattern on his arm. "Nothing really. Just making peace."

"Everything cool between you two now?" he asked. His instinct had been to go over and pull Bella away from Lucinda.

"Yes. This is going to sound kind of silly, but I think a lot of the blame was mine. I felt so…naked when it happened that I didn't really give Lucinda or my other friends a chance to reject me. I just shut down. And then my mother ended up working for some of them, which was very awkward."

He held her closer, rubbing his hand up and down her back. He loved how fragile she felt in his arms. It made him feel that he could protect her. And he wanted to do that, he realized, not just physically but also emotionally. He didn't want anyone to snub her or make her feel less than worthy.

"I can understand that. What changed now?"

"You changed me," she said softly. Her fingers moved from his arm to the buttons of his shirt. She toyed with the open button at his collar and then opened a second one, slipping her hand under the fabric to caress his chest.

He arched one eyebrow at her. "How did I do that?"

He was trying to keep his mind on the conversation, but his blood seemed to be flowing heavier in his veins.

"I think it was the way you accepted me and Dare. The way you were never condescending to us." She circled his nipple with her fingertip, scratching her nail around it. He groaned deep in his throat.

"Money doesn't mean everything," he said, but a part of him knew that wasn't what he really believed. Their entire relationship was based on finances. He'd given her his contacts and entrée back into the world she wanted to belong to.

She shifted on his lap.

"It does to some people," she said.

He didn't want to talk any longer. He wanted her naked, he wanted to open the birthday present he'd been planning on savoring all day long.

He tugged at the hem of her camisole top, but she caught his wrists in her hands. "Not yet."

She hopped off his lap. When he moved to stand she pushed him back to the glider.

"Wait here. I have a present for you."

"You don't need to give me anything else. I'll be happy to undress you and count that as the best present I've received."

She smiled at him with her heart in her eyes and he had trouble swallowing. "You can do that after you open my other gift."

She left him alone on the porch while she went inside. A few minutes later he heard the sound of a Jimmy Buffett ballad—"Stars Fell on Alabama"—and then she reappeared. She held a small box in her hands.

He took it, recognizing the blue box with the white ribbon. He knew she was on a budget and worried that she might have given him something too extravagant.

"Open it," she said.

He did, and saw a pair of silver fish cuff links. Masculine, understated. He looked up at her. Perfect.

"I know how you love the sea and being out on your boat," she said.

He realized then that he'd fallen for her. And he didn't like it. Didn't like the power she had over him. The intense vulnerability that feeling brought with it.

He suddenly felt unworthy of her. Everything he had in his life had been given to him due to the lucky circumstances of his birth. Bella had lost everything, then carved a life and a place for herself in the world through sheer determination.

If he'd learned anything tonight, it was that he couldn't let her go. And watching his parents had strengthened his resolve to never ruin his relationship with Bella by marrying her.

Eleven

Bella's day wasn't going according to plan. Tomorrow was the official last day on her contract with Jeremy and she wanted to put the finishing touches on the private event she'd been working on for the two of them.

But instead of focusing on Jeremy, she had to turn her attention to her business. And for the first time, she really resented it.

Her business had always been the center of her life, the thing she used to keep herself on track and balanced.

But now Jeremy filled that need.

They'd had brunch with his mother and aunt

Mary on Sunday, merging their lives even more closely together, and she'd found that she liked that. She'd arrived at work today feeling hopeful.

Now Shelley had been in a minor fender bender and was late for work. One of Shelley's clients had shown up early, while the client Bella was supposed to be meeting with was late.

She smiled at Huntley Donovan of the Art Council Guild as she showed her to the conference room and left to get her something to drink.

Randall, one of her event managers, walked in the door. Bella pounced on him. "Thank God you're here. Shelley was in an accident. She's fine, but she was supposed to be doing a precontract bid for the Art Guild this morning."

"I know. That's why I'm here. She called me before she called her insurance agent."

Randall was one of her best employees. He'd joined her staff only three months earlier and had proven himself invaluable. He was a tall African-American man with an easy smile and affable charm as well as a sense of calmness that put even the most temperamental clients at ease.

"I think it's time I gave her a raise," Bella said with a smile.

"Where is Ms. Donovan?"

"In the conference room. She'd like a cup of Earl Grey tea, and the file is somewhere on Shelley's desk," she said, gesturing toward the messy stack of paper.

Randall walked over to the desk and started going through the piles there. "I've got it."

"Thanks, Randall. I'm expecting a new client any minute."

Her phone was ringing when she entered her office and she was almost afraid to answer it and have one more thing go wrong.

"Good morning, this is Isabella."

"Hey, honey. Got a few minutes?" Her pulse sped up just at the sound of his voice. Oh, man, she had it bad for him. She propped her hip on the edge of her desk so she could keep an eye on the front door for her client.

"Yes. My client is running a few minutes late," she said, trying to reach her coffee cup while they were talking. It was too far away. With anyone else she'd put the phone down and grab her coffee but she didn't want to miss anything that Jeremy said.

"I want you to clear your calendar for tonight and tomorrow."

That arrogance of his was going to get him in trouble someday, but not today. She did like the way he was so confident in everything he said and did with her.

"I'll try," she said, adding that task to the growing to-do list in her head. Frankly, after this morning, she wanted to take a few weeks off and just hide away.

"Don't try. I need you to do it."

"Is this more than mere bossiness?" she asked.

There was a tone in his voice that she'd never heard before. Something she couldn't place.

"Yes."

"What's up?" she asked. "Is everything okay with your family?"

"Yes. I have something special planned for tonight and I think we're going to want to spend the day together tomorrow."

"What do you have planned?" she asked. She should have realized that he'd be as aware as she was that they were nearing the end of their contracted time together.

"Something special that's just for you," he said. There was an odd huskiness to his voice.

"Another surprise? I think I'm beginning to like them." And she was. Before Jeremy, she'd liked to know every detail of her day and any variation would immediately send her into crisis mode. But she'd learned that not every upheaval was a bad one. Not every surprise was to be dreaded. In fact, most of the ones he'd sprung on her were to be embraced.

"You'll like this one."

"Promise?" she asked, knowing that was just her knee-jerk reaction. Her conditioned response to anything unexpected.

"Guarantee it, honey."

"I'm going to hold you to that."

"You do that. I'll pick you up around six tonight."

"Where are we going?"

"Out on my yacht."

They hadn't been out on his yacht since the night they'd had that argument and he'd said that he didn't want their time together to end. She told herself not to get her hopes up, not to expect more than he'd promised her. But she felt a tinge of excitement.

"What are we going to be doing?"

"Having dinner and discussing the future."

A surge of joy went through her and she could hardly speak as he said goodbye. She hung up the phone, her mind alive with the possibilities of what the future held for her and Jeremy.

Jeremy checked every inch of the yacht before leaving to pick up Bella. Andy had prepared Bella's favorite meal and left him explicit instructions for heating it up. He'd had the housekeeping staff ensure that the dining room was set to Jeremy's exact instructions.

The bed was made up with the new Egyptian cotton sheets he'd ordered that would just match Bella's honey-brown eyes.

He had her favorite white wine chilling in the fridge, her favorite songs queued up on his Bose stereo. In fact, everything was as perfect as he could make it. He adjusted one of the blooms in the vase of purple tulips before he climbed the stairs two at a time and vaulted from the boat to the dock. He could probably run all the way to her house and not get rid of the excess energy that was dogging him tonight.

Seldom was he nervous about anything, but he was about tonight. He had played the scenario in his head a million times during the last few days. He'd gone over every possible answer she could give him and had a contingency plan worked out for each one.

He forced himself to stand still and calm the nervous energy. This was the same as closing a big deal at the office. Except a big deal never affected him this way. He had a lot invested in the outcome of this evening. He'd done everything he could to ensure he got the outcome he wanted.

Then why the hell was he so nervous?

He shook his head at his own stupidity and walked to his car. Once he had Bella on his boat out at sea, everything would fall into place.

He knew she wanted to be with him. She'd said as much the last time they were here. And he knew she needed some kind of stability, so his plan was absolutely perfect.

He drove to her home and parked out front, waiting for a few minutes before getting out. He refused to give in to the urge to get to her sooner. He had to manage his emotional response to her and so far, tonight, he was doing a piss-poor job of it.

He rang the bell instead of letting himself in with

the key she'd given him. He liked her quiet neighborhood more than he'd expected to. One of her neighbors waved at him as she backed out of her driveway. It seemed like a good sign. A sign that things were meant to be between him and Bella.

The door opened with a rush of cold air. He glanced at Bella, his words dying on his lips. She was breathtaking in her simple silk sundress. The halter top dipped down in the front between her breasts.

"Aren't you going to say anything?" she asked, looking like a femme fatale.

"Uh-huh," he said, but he couldn't get his brain to work. Her hair was pulled up on top of her head and a few tendrils fell around her face.

She had on some kind of dewy lip gloss that made him ache to lick her lips. To taste them. He skimmed his gaze higher and saw the amusement in her eyes. He knew he was a goner.

He stepped forward, put his hand on the back of her head and tilted her head up to his. He leaned down and licked at her lips. They tasted sweet but when he thrust his tongue into her mouth, he realized he liked the way she tasted more. Craved her on his tongue.

His body stirred. He thrust her away from him, turning his back to her before he did something crazy like make love to her on the front-hall table.

"Jeremy?"

"Bella...dammit, woman, I have plans for this evening."

"Ah, sorry?"

He shook his head and cleared his throat and then turned around again. "Good evening. You look gorgeous tonight."

"Thanks. You look very nice as well," she said. There was a lightness about her tonight that he'd never seen before and as soon as he recognized it, he was at ease. She wasn't on her guard around him.

"I hope this is okay," she said.

"I have no idea what you're talking about," he said.

"My clothes. You said it was going to be a special evening, so I thought I'd dress up."

"I like you dressed up," he said. The only thing he liked more was her naked. But her clothing tonight was perfect for what he had in mind. He was glad she'd picked up on the vibe he'd sent her. Glad to see that she, too, was ready for a special night.

When he'd asked her to be his mistress he had no idea how important she'd become to his life.

"I thought you would. Do we have time for a drink before we leave?" she asked.

"We're going out on the boat so we have all the time we'd like."

"So, do you want a drink?" she asked.

"I want this evening to be perfect for you, Bella."

"I think it will be," she said, pushing the door all the way open. "Come on in."

He followed her into her home and saw she'd taken the time to prepare for this drink. She had all the ingredients for his favorite cocktail on her bar. She mixed him a Grey Goose martini and poured it neatly into a glass, then garnished it with a cocktail onion instead of an olive. Then she poured herself one as well.

"To the future," she said with a faint smile.

"The future," he said, tapping their glasses together.

He watched her take a sip of the cool drink and tip her head to the side to watch him. He knew there was no such thing as a sure thing, but he felt very sure of Bella.

Very sure that he'd made the right decision as far as tonight went.

The sun was setting as they left the marina behind. Bella relaxed against the padded bench at the back of the yacht while Jeremy piloted the boat. Her entire body was buzzing from the way he'd kissed her when he'd shown up at her door.

They'd talked on the way to the yacht club, but not about anything important. Just the day's events. And it was nice to be able to share that with someone. She'd never really had that before Jeremy. Dare asked how she was, but he didn't really listen unless something was wrong that she needed him to attend to.

It was so different with Jeremy. She had given up cautioning herself about expecting too much from him. She was filled with the love she felt for him. It made her nerves tingle.

She wanted him. Needed him. Needed to be by his side.

Kicking off her high-heeled sandals, she walked across the deck to him. The breeze tugged at her hair and a few more strands escaped her clip. She felt them curling over her bare shoulders. Finally she reached him and she wrapped her arms around his back, resting her head between his shoulder blades.

He turned in her arms, lowering his head to hers. She lifted her face, meeting him halfway. The kiss was everything she wanted, yet left her wanting more.

She framed his face with her hands as he moved his mouth over hers, skimming his tongue along the seam of her lips and then pushing inside. He tasted wild and untamed, like the sea surrounding them. He groaned and angled his head for a deeper penetration of her mouth.

He pulled her body more tightly against his. She felt the weight of her breasts against his chest and his big hands wrapped around her waist. She stroked his face and neck with her hands. He lifted her more fully into him.

His kiss left room for nothing but thoughts of

Jeremy. His hands slid down her back, pulling her closer. He nibbled on her mouth and she felt like she was completely at his mercy.

Exactly where she wanted to be. She dug her nails into his shoulders as she leaned up, brushing against his chest.

She glanced down and saw her nipples pressing against the thin bodice of her dress. Jeremy skimmed his thumbs over her breasts before he slid his hands beneath the fabric.

"Baby, you are playing hell with my plans."

"Should I go sit back down?"

"Oh, hell, no," he said, caressing her back and spine.

She had a feeling she was going to remember this night for the rest of her life.

Jeremy dropped anchor when they were in the middle of nowhere. They were out of shipping lanes and away from other boats. The moon had risen and the sky stretched forever, enveloping them both in the night.

His body still pulsed from making love to Bella, and he wanted her again. He wanted to take her down to his bed and have her again and again until she forgot every name except his.

But first he wanted to ask her to stay with him.

She'd gone down to the master stateroom a few minutes earlier to touch up her makeup. He hoped she reapplied that slick lip gloss. He was looking forward to kissing it off again.

He went into the galley and readied their meal, then took out the presents he'd purchased for her, setting them in the different areas where he needed them.

He took a deep breath. He was a little nervous about her reaction no matter how well he thought he'd planned for it. He wanted her in his life for a long time. This was what he needed. What they both needed.

He opened the bottle of wine and left it to breathe and then checked the drawer where he'd left the paperwork he'd need later if she agreed to his proposition.

"What's that?"

He shut the drawer and turned to look at her. She'd taken her hair down and it hung in waves over her shoulders. She had reapplied her lip gloss and her dress was refastened. In the center of the V-neck he noticed a mark he'd left on her.

He took a box off the counter. "This is for you."

She glanced again at the drawer but took the gift and let the other matter drop. He poured her a glass of wine, then leaned one hip against the counter and just watched her.

"You're making me nervous."

He shrugged, taking a sip of his wine. "I like looking at you."

"I like having you look at me," she said, a hint of shyness in her voice.

"How can you be shy with me after all we've done together?" he asked, coming over to stand next to her.

"I don't know. It's different when we're together. I forget about everything else."

"Good. Now open your present so we can have dinner."

She opened it. He heard the gasp of surprise in her voice and he was pleased. He took the diamond and sapphire pendant necklace from the box.

"Hold your hair up," he said.

She lifted her hair and he fastened the necklace. Keeping his hands on her neck, he leaned down and kissed her. He wanted to find a way to tell her everything that was inside him even though he knew he couldn't.

He lifted his head slowly and took her arm, escorting her to the dining area. He picked up the gift-wrapped box by her seat.

"Open this one while I'm getting our dinner."

"Jeremy, you spoil me."

"It's about time someone did," he said. He ached for her past and her childhood. The way it had been torn away from her. He wanted to make sure that she had a safe cocoon for the rest of her life. That she never again had to face financial insecurity or worry about being left alone.

That's why his plan would work for both of them. It was a safe way for them to be together and not have to worry about the unexpected things that life sometimes threw at them.

He dished up their food and brought the plates over to the table. She'd opened the second present, a bracelet that matched the necklace he'd just given her.

She fastened it around her wrist and glanced up at him. There was so much hope in her eyes that it was almost painful to glimpse it.

He knew he had to do this right. He couldn't screw this up for her. Her trust was a precious gift and he didn't want to abuse it.

"Thank you for the bracelet, Jeremy. I wish I had something to give you."

"You already did."

"Sex?"

"No, Bella. So much more than that. Ralph Waldo Emerson once said that 'the only true gift is a portion of yourself.' You've given me a gift that I can never reciprocate. Bringing me into the circle of your friends. Welcoming me into your life and into your bed."

Tears glittered in her eyes and he thought, yes, this was right. For once he was doing what he needed to do. He wasn't betting on charm to get him through, but speaking straight from his gut.

"That is the sweetest thing anyone has ever said to me."

"It's only the truth."

The conversation ranged over many topics as they ate, and soon Jeremy was clearing the dishes away. He brought out a fruit-and-cheese tray with a small box nestled on it.

He handed her the box after he seated himself.

"I have something I want to ask you, Bella. But first please open this last present."

Bella held her breath as she opened the box. She could hardly concentrate on the gift, wanting instead to know what he was going to ask her. Would it be to marry him?

After brunch last Sunday with his family, she suspected he had something permanent in mind for the two of them. And she wanted that. She'd already made up her mind to ask him to move in with her after their contract was up.

"Bella, open the box," he said.

She did and found a pair of teardrop earrings that matched the necklace and bracelet he'd already given her. Jeremy was at his most romantic tonight. And she couldn't help falling more deeply in love with him.

He was everything she'd ever wanted in a man. Caring, attentive, supportive and the kind of lover every woman dreamed of having. She glanced up to find him watching her. She removed the silver hoop earrings she had on and put on the ones that matched her necklace and bracelet.

Was a matching ring soon to follow?

"Thank you."

"You're welcome, honey."

She didn't want to rush him but he didn't say anything else, and finally she couldn't stand it any longer. "You said you had a question."

"I do. I'm not sure how to ask it."

"Whatever it is, just ask."

He leaned forward. "Do you remember when we met?"

How could she forget? Her secret crush noticing her at a party where she was working, taking the time to talk to her and flirt with her and then offering her something that could never be repaid. "Yes."

"From that moment, you've been like an obsession for me. The last three and a half years I've been consumed with thoughts of you."

"Oh, Jeremy," she said, unable to keep her emotions from her voice. It was like he had glimpsed inside her heart and knew what she felt for him. "Me, too."

He smiled at her then. It was a sweet expression and not one she'd ever seen before on his fierce face.

"Obsessions aren't healthy things because they are all or nothing. Our relationship was nothing at first, just a piece of paper that was kept in a file. But then it became...well, I think you'll agree it became more than either of us ever anticipated."

She'd never been a man's obsession before and

was flattered he'd thought about her so much. It made her feel a lot less vulnerable. It reminded her that Jeremy was invested in this relationship, too.

"I'd definitely agree to that," she said. She'd never expected to fall so completely in love with Jeremy. In the beginning she might have even intended to use him to get back into the crowd that had once been her own, but that had quickly faded. She wanted *him,* and it didn't matter if he was part of her old social set or not.

"I was hoping that you'd feel this way, Jeremy. For the last few weeks I've been dreading this day. Knowing that it would mean an end to our contracted time together."

He reached across the space between them and took her hands in his. She liked the way his big hands enfolded hers.

"Me, too. I've been thinking our situation over. Trying to come up with a new relationship that would suit us both."

"Anything where we can be together will work with me. I don't think I can take living apart now. You really have become so much a part of my life."

"I hoped you would say that."

He tugged her to her feet, drawing her to him. He led her upstairs. He hit a button and low-level lighting illuminated the deck. She saw that there were a bunch of pillows on the bench where they'd made love earlier.

"What are we doing up here?"

"I wanted to hold you in my arms," he said. He pushed a button and music came from the speakers. Not pop music, but Ella Fitzgerald, her evocative voice singing about love and heartbreak in a way that made Bella believe that the woman had experienced them. She rested her head on Jeremy's shoulder as he danced them around the deck.

In this moment everything felt perfect. The anticipation of his question hung between them, sweetening the moment. For the last few months she'd been so aware of the contract and the expiration date of their relationship, and now she felt something so magical she could scarcely comprehend that this moment was here.

When the song ended he pushed a button and the music stopped. He led her toward the railing of the boat and turned her in his arms so they both faced the distant horizon. He wrapped his arms around her and pulled her back into the cradle of his body. He surrounded her completely.

She took it all in—the moonlight on the water, the softly blowing salt-scented breeze. The rocking motion of the boat and the heat of the man standing behind her.

He took a deep breath. "This is so much harder than I thought it would be."

Suddenly she was afraid. But she took a deep breath and turned in his arms. "Whatever it is,

Jeremy, if it involves the two of us staying together, then my answer is going to be yes."

He crushed her to him in a hug that made her feel like he'd never let her go. "I'm so glad to hear that. I've had a new contract drawn up and it is more generous than our last agreement."

She pulled back to look at him. "What kind of contract? I thought we'd moved beyond needing some legal paperwork between us."

"Honey, I want to make sure that you're protected. That you have everything you've ever wanted."

That sounded so nice that she cautioned herself from letting her temper get the better of her. Maybe it was some kind of prenuptial agreement. The kind that Kell had been talking about these last few months. "Do you have the contract with you?"

"Yes, I do."

"Let me see it."

Bella heard Jeremy talking and knew he was saying something important, but for the life of her she couldn't understand what the heck it was. She followed him down the gangplank back to the dining room where the remains of their dessert still sat on the table.

The last five minutes had been so bizarre she was sure she'd entered some kind of twilight zone. He seemed normal, but maybe there'd been some kind of break in the time-space continuum that had put her in an alternate universe where the man she loved would offer her a contract to stay with him.

"Here's the contract," he said, handing her a folder with a thick sheaf of papers inside.

She took the folder from him and drifted over to the table. Sitting down, she opened it up and saw the words at the top that stopped her. This was the same shell agreement as the original mistress contract she'd signed three years ago.

Anger began a slow churning deep inside her and she used that anger to help stem the tears that wanted to flow. How could he have completely missed the point?

"I think you'll agree that the new contract is more generous than the first one was. I've recently started doing business with an international firm that I think will net you a lot of new contacts. I've offered that as well as an exclusive arrangement with my company to be our only party planner."

"Please don't say anything else," she said, forcing the words out in a reasonable tone. But inside she was screaming and she didn't think she was going to stop for a long time. This evening that had been picture-perfect had shattered into a million little pieces. Pieces that cut deeper than she would have thought they could. And hurt so badly she didn't feel like she was going to recover.

But she'd deal with that later. She just wanted to

keep it together until she could get away and be by herself so she could lick her wounds in private.

Once again she'd fallen for an illusion. Something she knew didn't exist for her. She wasn't one of those women who was meant to have a stable, happy future. She was meant to live one day at time.

"Bella? What's the matter, honey?"

She glanced up at him and realized that he meant this to be in both of their best interests.

She took a deep breath and fought to find the words she needed. "Why do you still want a contract?"

"It's the only way to make sure we're both protected. I know that you need financial security and I need..."

"What do you need?"

He shrugged and looked away from her.

"Jeremy, I don't want to be your mistress anymore."

"Is it that you doubt the business I can generate for you? I can add an addendum that guarantees at least a million dollars a year in new business for the length of the contract."

She shook her head and got to her feet. "I think you should take me home."

"Not yet. Talk to me, Bella. I'm willing to sweeten the deal."

Was he really? Was he just afraid to admit he cared for her without knowing where she stood? For a minute she stood there, undecided, afraid to take a chance. But then she remembered that life was precarious and changed on a dime. And this might really be her only chance at love.

"I don't want you for your contacts or the amount of business you can generate. I want you for you."

He frowned at her and rubbed the back of his neck. Crossing to the bar he poured himself a shot of whiskey and downed it in one gulp.

"Jeremy, don't you feel anything for me?"

"Obsession," he said, the one word bit out between drinks as he refilled his glass again.

His earlier words circled in her mind. She'd thought he was joking, but saw now that he viewed her as something unhealthy for him and his life. Less than worthy, she thought. Still not worthy of someone in that social set.

"You're an obsession for me, Bella. This is the only way I know how to control our relationship. I have to know the parameters."

"Why would you want that? We could have a really great relationship. The kind that most people only dream of. Why can't you see that?"

"These last six months haven't been realistic," he said. "We have the illusion of a relationship. Because we both know that it can't end until the contract runs out."

She couldn't believe what she was hearing. "Do you really think that what I feel for you is some by-product of the contract?"

He shrugged. "I don't want to analyze it too closely. Whatever you feel for me...whatever you tell yourself, that's all immaterial to the contract. I think we've both proven that we're trustworthy."

She felt tears stinging her eyes and this time had no anger to assuage them. She tried to say something else, but her mouth trembled and she couldn't make herself talk.

She'd thought she'd been hurt in all the ways a person could be. That her heart had been thoroughly broken. But until this minute, when she stood in front of the man she'd given her heart to and heard him describe her as contractually trustworthy, she realized she hadn't known how deeply love could hurt.

"I can't believe I fell in love with you."

"You aren't really in love with me," he said. "It's obsession, honey."

"I think I know the difference between love and obsession, Jeremy."

He didn't say anything else and finally she couldn't stand the silence between them for another second. "Please take me back to shore. I want to go home."

Twelve

Bella ignored the phone and her friends and concentrated only on business. But at the end of two weeks, even though she was utterly exhausted, she still couldn't sleep through the night. She'd gotten used to Jeremy's presence in her bed and in her life, and she missed him.

Even though he was a huge jackass with some stupid ideas about her and their relationship, she still missed him. That really ticked her off because it made her feel like an idiot. But in the middle of the night, when she stared out her window at the waning moon, she couldn't help but remember their last night together and how perfect it had been. Until he'd brought out the contract.

Her lack of sleep made her cranky at the office. Randall and Shelley had insisted she go home early. So here she was in the middle of the afternoon, sitting on her porch on the glider, Jack Johnson playing on her iPod and a cup of blueberry tea at her side.

She was putting together a bid for another event at the Norton and wanted to double-check the images from the last event. She absolutely refused to think of Chihuly glass ceilings or the exquisite sculpture that was now in her backyard.

She uploaded a batch of pictures from her digital camera, forgetting that she'd used it the night of Jeremy's thirty-fifth birthday until the images starting popping up on her computer screen.

She stared at them. At him. At the picture she'd snapped of him with Kell, both men looking intense and serious just standing in a corner talking.

"Jeremy," she said, hearing the heartache in her own voice.

She cropped the picture down so that it was just him. Soon his face filled her screen and she traced his eyebrows and the sun lines around his eyes. God, she missed him.

Maybe she should go back to him. Swallow her pride and say yes to his contract. Except she knew she could never be happy as his mistress. She wanted to be his wife. That was the truth of it.

She wished she'd had a friend who could have

offered her a bit of advice at the beginning of the original mistress contract—*don't fall in love.*

"Too late."

Lucinda had called her twice. Each time the messages had been short and to the point, just saying that she was there for Bella.

Her doorbell rang and she minimized the screen she'd been working on, setting her computer on the glider seat before going to answer the door.

She checked the peephole first and scowled as she recognized Kell. She opened the door and he frowned at her and then cursed under his breath.

"You look like hell."

"Uh, thanks." She pulled the jacket of her sweat suit closer together before crossing her arms over her chest. Randall and Shelley had pretty much said the same thing when they'd sent her home this afternoon.

"Damn, this is a mess. I thought I had everything figured out but I think I'm missing something here," Kell said, running his hand through his thick blond hair.

"What are you talking about? It's really too early in the day for you to be drunk."

"I don't drink. Listen, can I come in?" he asked, taking a step toward her before she could even move.

"Sure."

She wanted to pretend he was the last person she wanted to talk to but the truth was she was starved for news on how Jeremy was doing. She had even tried to delicately pump her brother for information, but Dare hadn't heard from Jeremy, either.

She led the way into her house, stopping in the middle of the living room. "What's up?"

He paced around the room like a caged tiger. There was a grim set to his mouth. "That's what I want to know."

"What did Jeremy tell you?" she asked, knowing that no one was going to be able to help them. Over the sleepless nights she'd spent alone in her bed, she'd rehashed everything a million times. She knew she couldn't force Jeremy to love her, and she didn't want to be with him without love.

"Nothing. He hasn't said a word about you in two weeks. All he does is work."

She shook her head. She wished he was getting on with his life, but by the same token a part of her was happy to hear she wasn't the only one suffering. It made her believe that maybe he had cared for her. "I'm sorry to hear that. I don't think it has anything to do with me."

"It has everything to do with you. It's clear to me that you two have had a fight. Whatever it was about, you need to go to him and fix it."

"It's not that easy."

"Yes, it is. No problems are that insurmountable."

"Some of them are, Kell. This isn't just a fight or a difference of opinion. We want different things from life."

Kell sighed. "I pushed him to offer you a prenup. Don't hold that against him."

"It wasn't that. I would sign one if he asked me to."

"Then what is it? He's so into you."

"He's not into me. At least not the way you mean. I'm an obsession that he's trying to exorcise from his soul."

"He said that?"

"Yes, he did. And I don't know how to convince him otherwise. I'm not sure what you want from me, but I can't just go back to him and pretend to be whatever he wants until he gets tired of me."

Kell stared at her for a long time. "Because you love him."

She nodded.

Kell paced over to the front door and opened it. Glancing back at her, he said, "Just think about talking to him."

She nodded and watched him leave, knowing that she'd think of little else other than Jeremy.

Jeremy watched the sunset from his multi-million-dollar home. He glanced around at the luxury furnishings and the life that was full of the best things money could buy. But it felt empty. It felt the way it had before he'd met Isabella McNamara and his life had changed.

Obsessions had a way of doing that.

But the thing was, he no longer believed she was only an obsession. Her words that last night on his boat haunted him. A million times he replayed them. Heard her say she loved him and then quietly ask to go home.

He'd broken her heart and he had no idea how to fix it. For a while he hadn't even contemplated fixing it. He'd wanted to find another woman and prove to Bella exactly how desirable he was to other females. But he'd been disinterested in any other woman.

Then this last week he'd realized how much she'd brought to his life. Not just her presence in his bed, but the way she'd brought his circle of friends together with hers. The effortless way she had of making connections between people and ensuring no one felt inferior.

The way she had long ago. And he'd offered her a contract to stay in his life. In retrospect, he understood perfectly where he'd gone wrong.

His gut said to go back to her and make another offer. One where she set the terms and he'd do whatever she wanted. Be her love slave or whatever else she'd have from him.

But another part, a bigger part, was truly afraid of what she made him feel. He'd hurt this past week in a way that he'd never felt before. His life had been a gilded one of privilege where no one denied him anything.

Until Isabella. His Bella. He wanted her back. He wanted her happy.

There was a knock on his study door before it opened. He glanced over his shoulder to see his butler standing in the doorway. "Are you receiving, sir?"

"Who is it, Thomas?" he asked, hoping against hope that it would be Bella. If she came to him, he'd take her back and throw out the contract.

"Kell, sir."

The last thing he wanted to do was talk to Kell, who kept trying to take the blame for his breakup by pointing out that some women found prenups offensive. If only he'd offered her a prenup, he had the feeling she would have signed it with no qualms. God, he'd been a total ass.

And Bella wasn't going to come back. She deserved a man who loved her the way she loved him.

She loved *him*. That's what she said. What if she'd been mistaken?

"Sir?"

He rubbed the back of his neck and glanced around the study. His desk was littered with files and he'd closed more deals this week than he had in the previous three months. He'd been working nonstop, jacked up on coffee and adrenaline. Afraid to close his eyes because he dreamed of her in his bed and woke aching and hungry for her.

"Yes, send him back."

Jeremy logged on to his e-mail while he was

waiting for Kell and saw that he had a message from Bella. Before he could open it, Kell came into the room and headed straight to the bar, grabbing a bottle of Perrier. "What the hell did you say to Bella?"

"Why?" he asked, distracted from her message for a moment by his cousin. Damn, he should have refused to see Kell—then he could have read her message in private.

"Because I went to see her to apologize for putting you up to asking for the prenup and…"

"And what?" He was surprised by Kell's actions, but he shouldn't have been. Kell had spent the last week telling him that just because he'd screwed up by trusting the wrong woman, Jeremy shouldn't screw up by not trusting the right woman.

"She looked like hell. I don't think she's slept in a week."

Dammit, he thought. He'd wanted to be her hero and to protect her. Instead he'd left her and she was worse off for having known him. "Leave it alone, Kell. I told you to stay away from her."

Kell didn't respond to that, just scooped some ice from the ice bucket and poured his Perrier into a glass. "You're miserable, too."

"And your point is?" he asked, trying not to look at his Outlook inbox, but failing. Why had she e-mailed him?

"You've never been stupid about anything. Not women, not business. Don't let her be the first."

"Why is this so important to you?"

"I want to believe that you and I can be happy."

"I'll take that under consideration," he said, glancing at his computer screen again.

"What's so important on your computer?"

"Bella sent me a message."

"Did you open it?"

"No, I'm waiting for you to leave."

"Are you sure you don't need me?"

He nodded. Kell walked toward the door. "I'll call you tomorrow."

Jeremy watched him go before finally clicking on the icon to open the e-mail message. It was brief and to the point. No smiley face after her name. Just a listing of JPEG file names.

Pictures from his birthday party. He opened them up one by one and felt like he'd been punched in the gut. In front of him in full color was the life he'd been afraid to imagine for himself and Bella. A life that was full of friends and family. One that they shared together.

And he knew then that there was a small chance that she still loved him. A woman who'd go through all this effort for her lover wasn't someone who could walk away easily. And he remembered other things she'd said that last night. Remembered that she, too, wanted a life together. Just not as his mistress.

Finally he got it.

He pushed away from his desk, grabbed his keys and walked out of his house. He didn't realize he was running until he reached his car.

The knock on her door just after dinner startled her. But a part of her had been hoping, ever since she'd e-mailed the pictures, that Jeremy would come. She was almost afraid to look in the peephole and see someone other than him.

But there he was. Wearing a pair of faded jeans and a faded college T-shirt. His hair was unkempt and he scarcely resembled the fashionable man she knew him to be.

She opened the door and stared at him. He didn't say anything to her, either. He shifted from one foot to the other.

"I got your e-mail."

"Oh. Did you like the pictures?"

"Yes. They turned out really nice," he said.

God, had he really come over here just to thank her for the pictures?

"I don't have any other ones."

"That's okay. Thanks for the ones you sent."

"You're welcome," she said, waiting for him to say something else, but minutes dragged by and he said nothing. Finally she realized that he wasn't going to say anything and a part of her was ready to beg him to take her back. But then she remembered how hard she'd struggled to rebuild her life. And she knew she couldn't. He had to meet her halfway.

"Goodbye, Jeremy," she said, starting to close the door.

His hand shot out and he blocked the door from closing. "Can I come in?"

"Why? To talk more about the photos?"

"No," he said, thrusting his hands through his hair. "I didn't come over here because of the pictures. I'm here because I'm an idiot."

"No, you're not."

"Yes, I am," he said, stepping over the threshold and closing the door behind him. "I want you in my life. I can't live without you."

"I want those things, too, but I don't want to be your mistress."

"I don't want that, either, not anymore. I was afraid to admit how much I need you, but that doesn't change the fact that I do need you, Bella. I'm asking you to take me back on your terms. I don't have a contract or gifts. I don't have anything except myself."

"Someone once told me that the best gift was one of yourself."

"A wise man."

She was almost afraid to hope that he meant what he said. "What if I said my terms were marriage and a family?"

"That offer would be more than I deserve," he said, drawing her into his arms and holding her so tightly she knew he'd never let go. "But I'd say yes before you changed your mind."

"I'm not going to change my mind."

"That's good." He buried his face against her neck. "I love you, Bella."

"I love you, too."

He lifted her in his arms and carried her into her bedroom. He made love to her and then cradled her to his chest. They talked about the future and made plans. Permanent plans. Plans for their life together.

* * * * *

Be sure to read the next sensual romance
in Katherine Garbera's THE MISTRESSES!
HIGH-SOCIETY MISTRESS
Available in July 2007
wherever Silhouette Books are sold.

THE ROYAL HOUSE OF NIROLI
Always passionate, always proud

The richest royal family in the world—united by blood and passion, torn apart by deceit and desire

Nestled in the azure blue of the Mediterranean Sea, the majestic island of Niroli has prospered for centuries. The Fierezza men have worn the crown with passion and pride since ancient times. But now, as the king's health declines, and his two sons have been tragically killed, the crown is in jeopardy.

The clock is ticking—a new heir must be found before the king is forced to abdicate. By royal decree the internationally scattered members of the Fierezza family are summoned to claim their destiny. But any person who takes the throne must do so according to The Rules of the Royal House of Niroli. Soon secrets and rivalries emerge as the descendents of this ancient royal line vie for position and power. Only a true Fierezza can become ruler—a person dedicated to their country, their people…and their eternal love!

Each month starting in July 2007,
Harlequin Presents is delighted to bring you
an exciting installment from
THE ROYAL HOUSE OF NIROLI,
in which you can follow the epic search
for the true Nirolian king.
Eight heirs, eight romances, eight fantastic stories!

Here's your chance to enjoy a sneak preview of the first book delivered to you by royal decree….

FIVE MINUTES later she was standing immobile in front of the study's window, her original purpose of coming in forgotten, as she stared in shocked horror at the envelope she was holding. Waves of heat followed by an icy chill surged through her body. She could hardly see the address now through her blurred vision, but the crest on its left-hand front corner stood out, its *royal* crest, followed by the address: *HRH Prince Marco of Niroli*...

She didn't hear Marco's key in the apartment door, she didn't even hear him calling out her name. Her shock was so great that nothing could penetrate it. It encased her in a kind of bubble, which only concentrated the torment of what she was suffering and branded it on her brain so that it could never be forgotten. It was only finally pierced by the sudden opening of the study door as Marco walked in.

"Welcome home, *Your Highness*. I suppose I ought to curtsy." She waited, praying that he would laugh and tell her that she had got it all wrong, that the envelope she was holding, addressing him as Prince Marco of Niroli, was some silly mistake. But like a tiny candle flame shivering vulnerably in the dark, her hope trembled fearfully. And then the look in Marco's eyes extinguished it as cruelly as a hand placed callously over a dying person's face to stem their last breath.

"Give that to me," he demanded, taking the envelope from her.

"It's too late, Marco," Emily told him brokenly. "I know the truth now…." She dug her teeth in her lower lip to try to force back her own pain.

"You had no right to go through my desk," Marco shot back at her furiously, full of loathing at being caught off guard and forced into a position in which he was in the wrong, making him determined to find something he could accuse Emily of. "I trusted you…."

Emily could hardly believe what she was hearing. "No, you didn't trust me, Marco, and you didn't trust me because you knew that I couldn't trust you. And you knew that because you're a liar, and liars don't trust people because they know that they themselves cannot be trusted." She not only felt sick, she also felt as though she could hardly breathe. "You are Prince Marco of Niroli…. How could you not tell me who you are and still live with me as intimately as we have lived together?" she demanded brokenly.

"Stop being so ridiculously dramatic," Marco demanded fiercely. "You are making too much of the situation."

"*Too much?*" Emily almost screamed the words at him. "When were you going to tell me, Marco? Perhaps you just planned to walk away without telling me anything? After all, what do my feelings matter to you?"

"Of course they matter." Marco stopped her sharply. "And it was in part to protect them, and you, that I decided not to inform you when my grandfather first announced that he intended to step down from the throne and hand it on to me."

"To protect me?" Emily nearly choked on her fury. "Hand on the throne? No wonder you told me when you first took me to bed that all you wanted was sex. You *knew* that was the only kind of relationship there could ever be between us! You *knew* that one day you would be Niroli's king. No doubt you are expected to marry a princess. Is she picked out for you already, your *royal* bride?"

* * * * *

Look for
THE FUTURE KING'S PREGNANT MISTRESS
by Penny Jordan in July 2007,
from Harlequin Presents,
available wherever books are sold.

HARLEQUIN®

Mediterranean
NIGHTS™

Experience the glamour and elegance of cruising the
high seas with a new 12-book series....

MEDITERRANEAN NIGHTS

Coming in July 2007...

SCENT OF A
WOMAN

by

Joanne Rock

When Danielle Chevalier is invited to an exclusive
conference aboard *Alexandra's Dream*, she knows it
will mean good things for her struggling fragrance
company. But her dreams get a setback when she
meets Adam Burns, a representative from a large
American conglomerate.

Danielle is charmed by the brusque American—
until she finds out he means to compete with her bid
for the opportunity that will save her family business!

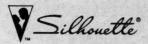

Silhouette®

Romantic
SUSPENSE

**Sparked by Danger,
Fueled by Passion.**

Mission: Impassioned

A brand-new miniseries begins with

My Spy

By *USA TODAY* bestselling author

Marie Ferrarella

She had to trust him with her life....
It was the most daring mission of Joshua Lazlo's
career: rescuing the prime minister of England's
daughter from a gang of cold-blooded kidnappers.
But nothing prepared the shadowy secret agent
for a fiery woman whose touch ignited something
far more dangerous.

My Spy
#1472

Available July 2007 wherever you buy books!

nocturne™

**DON'T MISS THE RIVETING CONCLUSION
TO THE RAINTREE TRILOGY**

RAINTREE: SANCTUARY

by *New York Times* bestselling author

BEVERLY
BARTON

Mercy, guardian of the Raintree
homeplace, takes a stand against
the Ansara wizards to battle for
the Clan's future.

*On sale July,
wherever books are sold.*

REQUEST YOUR FREE BOOKS!

2 FREE NOVELS PLUS 2 FREE GIFTS!

Passionate, Powerful, Provocative!

YES! Please send me 2 FREE Silhouette Desire® novels and my 2 FREE gifts. After receiving them, if I don't wish to receive any more books, I can return the shipping statement marked "cancel." If I don't cancel, I will receive 6 brand-new novels every month and be billed just $3.80 per book in the U.S., or $4.47 per book in Canada, plus 25¢ shipping and handling per book and applicable taxes, if any*. That's a savings of almost 15% off the cover price! I understand that accepting the 2 free books and gifts places me under no obligation to buy anything. I can always return a shipment and cancel at any time. Even if I never buy another book from Silhouette, the two free books and gifts are mine to keep forever.

225 SDN EEXJ 326 SDN EEXU

Name	(PLEASE PRINT)	
Address		Apt.
City	State/Prov.	Zip/Postal Code

Signature (if under 18, a parent or guardian must sign)

Mail to the **Silhouette Reader Service™**:
IN U.S.A.: P.O. Box 1867, Buffalo, NY 14240-1867
IN CANADA: P.O. Box 609, Fort Erie, Ontario L2A 5X3

Not valid to current Silhouette Desire subscribers.

Want to try two free books from another line?
Call 1-800-873-8635 or visit www.morefreebooks.com.

* Terms and prices subject to change without notice. NY residents add applicable sales tax. Canadian residents will be charged applicable provincial taxes and GST. This offer is limited to one order per household. All orders subject to approval. Credit or debit balances in a customer's account(s) may be offset by any other outstanding balance owed by or to the customer. Please allow 4 to 6 weeks for delivery.

Your Privacy: Silhouette is committed to protecting your privacy. Our Privacy Policy is available online at www.eHarlequin.com or upon request from the Reader Service. From time to time we make our lists of customers available to reputable firms who may have a product or service of interest to you. If you would prefer we not share your name and address, please check here. ☐

SDES07

COMING NEXT MONTH

#1807 THE CEO'S SCANDALOUS AFFAIR—
Roxanne St. Claire
Dynasties: The Garrisons
He needed her for just one night—but the repercussions of their sensual evening could last a lifetime!

#1808 HIGH-SOCIETY MISTRESS—Katherine Garbera
The Mistresses
He will stop at nothing to take over his business rival's company…including bedding his enemy's daughter and making her his mistress.

#1809 MARRIED TO HIS BUSINESS—Elizabeth Bevarly
Millionaire of the Month
To get his assistant back this CEO plans to woo and seduce her. But he isn't prepared when she ups the stakes on *his* game.

#1810 THE PRINCE'S ULTIMATE DECEPTION—
Emilie Rose
Monte Carlo Affairs
It was a carefree vacation romance. Until she discovers she's having an affair with a prince in disguise.

#1811 ROSSELLINI'S REVENGE AFFAIR—
Yvonne Lindsay
He blamed her for his family's misery and sought revenge in a most passionate way!

#1812 THE BOSS'S DEMAND—Jennifer Lewis
She was pregnant with the boss's baby—but wanted more than just the convenient marriage he was offering.

SDCNM0607